"You're traveling alone."

"I often do," Alicia said. "Again, I'm a grown woman. I can take care of myself. And if anyone tries to mess with me, I have a gun, remember?"

Harrison reared back. "On you?"

"In my bag. Would you like to see my concealed carry permit?"

"No." He shook his head, then had the good grace to laugh at himself. "I never thought of you carrying a weapon. Every time I've seen you, you've been more on the command side of things. I thought you were a suit. Like me," he added with a winsome smile.

"I am," she said, amused. "But I'm also armed at all times."

He chuckled and shook his head. "I'm not sure if I should be terrified or turned on," he admitted.

"I recommend both," she answered without hesitation.

TRIAL IN THE BACKWOODS

—

MAGGIE WELLS

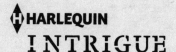

For my Super Cool Party People—my life would truly suck
without you.

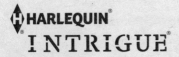

H HARLEQUIN®
INTRIGUE®

Recycling programs
for this product may
not exist in your area.

ISBN-13: 978-1-335-48917-3

Trial in the Backwoods

Copyright © 2021 by Margaret Ethridge

This edition published by arrangement with Harlequin Books S.A.

For questions and comments about the quality of this book,
please contact us at CustomerService@Harlequin.com.

Harlequin Enterprises ULC
22 Adelaide St. West, 40th Floor
Toronto, Ontario M5H 4E3, Canada
www.Harlequin.com

Printed in U.S.A.

By day **Maggie Wells** is buried in spreadsheets. At night she pens tales of intrigue and people tangling up the sheets. She has a weakness for hot heroes and happy endings. She is the product of a charming rogue and a shameless flirt, and you only have to scratch the surface of this mild-mannered married lady to find a naughty streak a mile wide.

Books by Maggie Wells

Harlequin Intrigue

A Raising the Bar Brief

An Absence of Motive
For the Defense
Trial in the Backwoods

Visit the Author Profile page at Harlequin.com.

CAST OF CHARACTERS

Harrison Hayes—The district attorney for Masters County and a soon-to-be father. About to try the biggest case of his career. If he doesn't get killed first.

Alicia Simmons—DEA special agent responsible for the sting operation that snagged Samuel Coulter. Determined to keep the DA safe to see her and Harrison's child born.

Ben Kinsella—Former DEA agent turned county sheriff.

Marlee Masters—The town golden girl, who has reinvented herself as the town business mogul.

Simon Wingate—Scion of Georgia's political family. Former defense attorney for Samuel Coulter.

Lourdes (Lori) Cabrera—Masters County sheriff's deputy whose dogged pursuit of Samuel Coulter led to his arrest.

Samuel Coulter—The eccentric millionaire and self-proclaimed naturalist about to stand trial on charges of drug and human trafficking.

Chapter One

The town of Pine Bluff hadn't changed much in the weeks since Alicia Simmons packed her bag and headed back to Atlanta, but she had. Only a couple of months ago, she'd been riding high on the arrest of one of the most insidious heroin traffickers in the southeastern United States. Heck, one week ago, she was the kind of woman who had a handle on exactly who she was and what she wanted. Sure, the promotion she'd thought was hers went to yet another member of the boys' club, but she couldn't honestly say she was shocked. Her path to section chief was littered with the prone bodies of men who thought they were better than she was. Time and again, she proved them wrong.

But she hadn't counted on getting pregnant.

So here she was, back in Pine Bluff, a million butterflies and one tiny embryo swirling in her belly. She hadn't intended to make the drive south. Now she sat parked at the curb in front of Harrison Hayes's neat ranch-style house.

She'd made a somewhat awkward call to her old

friend Ben Kinsella to get the address, burbling something about wanting to add Hayes to her Christmas card list. The former DEA agent turned county sheriff threw her for a loop when he complained about how he'd never received a Christmas card from her in all the years they'd been acquainted. The torment had been cut short, though. Ben's girlfriend, Marlee Masters, had snatched the phone from the nosy sheriff and provided Hayes's address with a minimum of fuss. Marlee, being the smart woman she was, also rattled off Ben's, though Alicia was fairly sure the other woman suspected no cards were being mailed.

Warm air blasted through the vents. December was only a couple of days off and the South Georgia evening had turned cool. Of course, this close to the Florida state line, it rarely ever got truly cold. Or if it did, not for long. Unlike the vicious winters she'd endured growing up in Wisconsin.

Drawing a bracing breath, she turned off the engine and opened the door. The brisk wind stung her cheeks and made her eyes water. Then again, they'd been watering nonstop since the day she realized she'd missed a period. Not because she was sad or even upset. More, she was surprised. She wasn't the type to enjoy surprises.

Pulling her jacket close around her, she circled the hood of the car and stepped onto the brick walkway leading to the small porch. She had a vague recollection of her previous visit. She'd been one too many tequila shooters in to appreciate the softness of the gunmetal-gray shutters against the white brick. What looked to be window boxes affixed to the front of the house held a few scraggly purple-and-yellow pansies. The lawn was mowed and edged. A smattering of crisp fall leaves dotted the expanse of yellowing green. Alicia figured they had to have blown in from a neighbor's yard, because the tall poplar planted in the center of Hayes's lawn was mostly bare.

Harrison Hayes was the orderly type. Not a shock. So was she. Normally. At least she wouldn't be the only one whose world was about to be shaken like a snow globe.

Stepping onto the porch, she shoved her hands deep into her pockets, giving herself one last chance to dissect her own motivation in coming here with news like this. She hadn't gotten pregnant on purpose. And though they both may have been tipsy the night eccentric millionaire Samuel Coulter was formally arraigned on drug- and human-trafficking charges, neither of them was anywhere close to being incapacitated. They'd willingly fallen into bed with each other. They were both aware of the added risk of having unprotected sex.

After all, they were adults. Responsible adults in positions of authority. More than most, they saw the day-to-day ramifications of bad choices. Why had they thought they were impervious?

Before she could change her mind, Alicia jerked her right hand out of her pocket and jabbed her index finger at the doorbell. A shiver ran down her spine. Something crackled under her foot. She looked down and spotted a brown mailing envelope left on the welcome mat. She swooped down to pick it up, peeking through the sidelights for any sign of occupancy. There were lights on in the house and a BMW parked in front of the closed garage door, but the presence of the car didn't necessarily mean he was home. In a town the size of Pine Bluff, residents often walked to their destinations. He could've taken a stroll downtown or—

The door opened and Harrison Hayes appeared, breathless and rumpled, wearing only a faded University of Georgia T-shirt, black gym shorts and an expensive-looking pair of athletic shoes. Alicia took in the sight for a moment. Harrison Hayes all sweaty and pumped up was something a woman should take time to appreciate.

"Alicia," he panted, his eyes widening. "What are you doing here?"

A valid question. All the way down from Atlanta, she'd debated her approach. One option would be to play it casual. Use the old "Oh, I was in town" line, but she dismissed the idea because neither of them was the type to simply drop by someone's house.

On the other end of the spectrum, she could blow in like a woman on a mission. As a special agent for the US Drug Enforcement Agency, storming in was a modus operandi she was far more familiar with, but she wasn't certain he deserved to have his life raided. Yes, choices were made, but they were made on both sides. She wasn't about to square off and demand he have answers for questions she hadn't fully wrapped her head around yet.

Tucking her chin to her chest, she slumped down into the collar of her coat, then gave her head a bewildered shake. "I, uh—"

A line formed between his dark brows, but there was no hesitation when he reached for her arms. Grasping her biceps, he pulled her into the house. Heat closed in around her, and for the first time since she'd seen the plus sign appear on the stick, something warm blazed low inside her.

"Are you okay?" he asked, running his hands up and down her arms like he might ward off any chill she might have caught.

"I'm fine," she replied. But it was a lie.

If she were fine, she wouldn't be there. If everything were okay, she'd be in Atlanta. If her whole world hadn't shifted on its axis, she probably never would have seen Harrison Hayes again. But here she was.

She thrust out the envelope she'd been clutching and pressed it to his chest. "You had a delivery."

"Come on inside," he ordered, gesturing toward the living room beyond the small foyer. He gently removed the envelope from her grasp, then guided her into the room. "I'm sorry it took me a minute to answer. I heard the doorbell but figured it was a warning."

"A warning?"

He gave a mirthless laugh. "Around here, doorbells are more a formality than anything. People ring them, but they usually walk on in. I figured you were Ben or Simon, but when you didn't come to the back, I thought I'd better check."

She let her gaze travel down over his workout attire. "You have a gym in the back?"

He shrugged. "I have a treadmill and some weights. Not exactly a gym, but it keeps me busy on cold nights." He pinched the fabric of her jacket between his thumb and forefinger. "Where are my manners? May I take your coat?"

Her lips quirked up. She forgot he was like this. The courtly Southern gentility must have been drilled into him growing up. And though she never got used to it, Alicia was surprised to discover she actually liked his old-fashioned demeanor. There was no condescension in him. No pretense. He simply wanted to make her more comfortable.

"Thank you," she said, slipping the jacket from her shoulders.

He caught it and held the collar as she extracted her arms. With the jacket draped over his forearm, he gestured for her to have a seat on a sleek low-slung sofa.

"Can I get you something to drink? Water? A beer? Or maybe you'd like something hot. I have coffee, but I don't think I have any tea in the house."

Her eyebrows rose. "No tea in the house? How will you ever survive?"

He chuckled. "I have iced tea, but no hot. There's a gallon of Bubba's in the refrigerator if you'd like iced tea."

The offer made her laugh. Only a true Southerner kept cold tea on hand at all times. Everywhere else in the world, it was a summer drink, but down here it was a way of life. And, according to Marlee Masters, only a single Southern man would buy the stuff they sold in the grocery store by the gallon.

Alicia desperately wanted a cup of coffee, but she didn't dare expose her unborn child to her caffeine addiction any more than she already had. "Water would be nice, thank you."

"Coming right up."

She watched him disappear around a corner to what she assumed was the kitchen. Asking for a drink was a stalling tactic, but she was having a hard time feeling ashamed. Seeing him again had thrown her.

In her mind, Harrison Hayes was no different from any other lawyer. Another brown-haired man in a nice suit with polished shoes and a briefcase. Line him up with a handful of other upper-middle-class businessmen and he'd blend right in.

Or so she'd thought.

She'd forgotten about the flecks of green and gold in his hazel eyes. She'd forgotten the way his square jaw looked covered in a true five-o'clock shadow. He was a clean-shaven man who fought a battle against growth lesser men cultivated and manicured with clippers. He was courtly and gallant, but he was also all man.

It was no stretch to imagine Hayes tromping off to the woods outfitted in camouflage and carrying a hunting rifle. Most of the men around these parts were avid hunters, inclined to spend their every autumn weekend buried deep in the deer woods or hiding out in a duck blind.

When he reappeared a moment later, she tried to gather her thoughts, but her runaway mouth betrayed her. "Do you hunt?"

He drew up short beside her seat, his brow creased into extremely attractive furrows of concentration when he bent forward and offered her a glass of water.

"Do I hunt?" he repeated.

Feeling foolish, but unable to abandon the line of questioning she'd begun, she said, "I wondered..." She glanced around the comfortably furnished living area and saw no evidence of trophy animals, but for all she knew, the man might have a rec room decorated with duck paneling and dozens of mounted deer heads. "I mean, it's hunting season in a lot of places," she continued. "I was only...asking."

The corner of his mouth quirked up, but rather than tease her about the odd inquiry, he simply shook his head. "No. I mean, I have hunted, but it's not my thing. I prefer fishing."

Alicia nodded, digesting this information and filing it away for future use. "I enjoy fishing too," she blundered on, happily latching on to any excuse not to approach the subject at hand. "Of course, I mainly fly-fish. Though I have also hauled in some crappie and walleye." He watched her with a bemused expression.

Hayes took a sip of his own water and smiled. "Then we have something in common. Except for the walleye. Don't see many of those around these parts."

Wetting her lips, she stiffened her spine and marshaled all of the nerve she usually reserved for storming into drug dealers' lairs. "I came here because I need to tell you something," she began haltingly.

Placing her glass on the coffee table, she leaned forward, rubbing her palms together between her knees and searching for the right words. "Hayes, I realize we don't know each other—"

She was called up short when he raised his hand and interrupted. "Harrison. Or Harry, if you prefer." She looked at him blankly, and he gave a wry smile and a shrug. "We may not have spent much time learning everything about one another, but we *have* seen one another naked. Seems odd not to be on a first-name basis."

"Right." She barked a laugh. "Of course." Alicia drew to an abrupt stop, her momentum lost. She looked up at him from under her lashes, wondering exactly how she was going to break this kind of news to a man so forthright.

But then, forthright was the answer. She simply needed to tell him straight-out.

"Harrison," she tried, then winced at the formality. "Harry," she amended, and he smiled encouragingly. "I need to talk to you about something pretty important."

"I figured it would take something big to bring you to my doorstep." He took the seat opposite her, then nodded. "Go on."

She looked up and this time met his gaze directly. "I'm pregnant."

He froze. She'd seen deer standing in the middle of a busy highway looking completely nonplussed compared to the otherworldly stillness of Harrison Hayes. She couldn't blame him. She didn't think she moved a muscle for five full minutes after seeing the plus sign show up in the tiny window on the over-the-counter pregnancy test. Then, when she did spring into action, it was to repeat the process with the two other tests she'd bought. Each time, she'd read the results with the same bewilderment currently breaking through his immobility.

"Excuse me?" he managed to croak.

"I'm pregnant," she responded, purposefully keeping her tone even. One of them had to remain calm, and she'd already had hours to freak out. It was Harry's turn now.

"But—" He huffed a laugh and scrubbed a hand over his face. "I was going to ask how, but I have a grasp on the mechanics of it."

Alicia watched him warily, all the while trying not to think about how unmechanical it had been between them. *Explosive. White-hot. Reckless. Hungry.* Those words might have fit better. But she was hip to what he was asking. Even in their tequila-fueled throes of passion, they'd paused long enough to have "the talk." They were adults, after all, not hormonal teenagers.

They'd left the celebration at Coulter's former defense attorney Simon Wingate's house and gone back to the place she'd rented for less than two full weeks. Like this baby's conception, Samuel Coulter's arrest and arraignment happened faster than anyone anticipated. Neither had a condom handy, but both swore they were in good health. She'd been diagnosed with polycystic ovarian syndrome in her early twenties and given birth control pills to help regulate her hormones. But even without the pill, her condition carried a high risk of infertility.

All of this added up in her head to mean she was meant to have this baby. Driving down to Pine Bluff, informing Harrison Hayes of his impending paternity and absolving him of all adjacent responsibility seemed reasonable. Possibly even noble.

"You're pregnant," he stated flatly, breaking into her reverie.

"Yes."

He blinked as if he still couldn't quite believe what he was hearing. "I assume you're here to tell me I'm the father?"

"Yes."

"Yes," he repeated dully. Then he threw his hands wide, absolute incredulity contorting his handsome face into an almost comical leer. "You're pregnant and you're saying I am the father."

"I'm pregnant and you absolutely are the father," she confirmed, keeping her tone even and nonconfrontational.

"Holy—" He shot from his seat and began to pace, plowing one hand through his rumpled brown hair. He wrapped the other around his middle and swung away from her. "I can't… Are you…? Well, of course you are, or you would never have driven all the way down here, right?"

She let him ramble, bracing herself so it all rolled off her. Words spoken in shock could and should not be held against a person.

"I took three tests," she informed him. "I haven't been to the doctor yet, but all three were pretty clearly positive." She paused, then gestured toward the foyer. "I have them out in the car. I can go get them and show you," she offered.

He held up a hand to stop her when she began to rise. "No." He wagged his head hard. "I believe you." Then, settling his hand on the back of his neck, he kneaded the muscle there. "God help us both, I believe you."

"I didn't plan for this to happen," she started.

Harry whirled, his hazel eyes glinting gold when they met hers. "Of course you didn't, but it did, and now…" His long strides ate up the floor space. He stopped in his tracks when he spotted the envelope she'd collected from his welcome mat. "What's this?" He snatched the envelope from the chair where he'd dropped it. "Did you bring legal papers or something?"

Alicia recoiled. In all their previous encounters, she'd pegged Hayes as a cool cucumber. A man so watchful and laid-back, he hadn't even batted an eyelash when Samuel Coulter assaulted his own attorney. But she'd managed to get such a levelheaded man utterly riled up one night, and it was a memory she reveled in for weeks after. But now, as she watched him grasp the craft-paper envelope in both hands and pull it apart at the seams, she wondered at her own powers of agitation.

"That wasn't mine—"

The first thing she noticed was the sheaf of blank white papers tumbling to the floor at his feet and scattering on the polished pine floors with a whoosh. When she looked up, she saw a dissipating cloud surrounding Harry's head and the streaks of white powder clinging to his clothes.

"Don't move," she shouted, springing to her feet.

"Don't come near me," he barked at the same time, thrusting his hands out to keep her at bay.

"Don't talk. Don't move, but don't hold your breath," she ordered, her training kicking in. "Breathe carefully. Keep it slow and shallow." She saw his chest expand and contract and moved directly into his line of sight, but outside the reach of his outstretched arms. "Let go of the envelope. Open your fingers and drop it."

To her relief, his fingers unclenched and it fell to the floor with the blank pages.

"Okay. Stay calm and don't move," she said in the same deliberately steady tone she'd used to deliver her big news. The soothing cadence employed by people who specialized in hostage negotiation.

"I'm not moving." But even as he spoke, he started to curl his arms in as if to reach for his shirt.

"Keep your arms as far away from the rest of your body as you can, but lift them over your head," she said, reaching for her purse.

"What? Why?" He shied away, but she plunged her hand into her bag and fumbled past her gun and credentials for a pair of the disposable gloves she always carried.

"Hold still." She wriggled her hands into the gloves and slid her fingers under the T-shirt, pushing her palms over his chest, spreading her wrists wide when she reached the neckband. She stretched the cotton until the threads popped. "Close your eyes. Close your mouth. Don't breathe. I have to get this over your head."

"What are you doing?"

"I've got to get you out of these clothes," she said urgently.

Chapter Two

In the weeks since Alicia Simmons blew out of Pine Bluff with her biggest bust to date on her résumé, Harrison Hayes had thought about her far more than he cared to admit. Their night together had been, for want of a better word, unforgettable.

They didn't simply have chemistry together. They created spontaneous combustion. But it didn't slow her roll. Barely forty-eight hours after the arraignment celebration ended with the two of them tangled in faded floral sheets, she was gone.

Now she was back. Here. Claiming to be pregnant. Next moment, there was white powder exploding all over his face, and she was trying to strip him naked in his own living room.

"You need to what?" he asked again, partially because he wasn't sure he'd heard her quite right, but mainly because he wanted her to have to say it again.

Despite the emotional tsunami her announcement had stirred, he couldn't say he was entirely opposed to her removing his clothes. Sure, she'd bruised his ego when she left without saying goodbye. But he had gone a long time without meeting anyone half as intriguing as she was, so he had no regrets. To pin his visceral reaction to her strictly to a lack of female companionship would be a lie. And Harrison made it a point not to lie to himself. Nor was he inclined to let her make a fool of him.

"Cooperate, please."

"Stop groping me," he ground out.

"Your face and clothes have been dusted with a suspect white powder," she said, speaking slowly and deliberately. Like he didn't have the brains to grasp his current situation. And she may have been justified in doing so. He wasn't having a hard time hearing her. Hell, he could hear his shirt tear when she stretched it farther and farther with the backs of her hands. He couldn't believe after all these weeks, she'd come into his house wanting to strip him naked, and it wasn't for recreational purposes.

"We need to get you out of these clothes and into the shower ASAP." She looked him dead in the eye. "Now, close your eyes and mouth, and do your best not to breathe in. I'm going to lift this over your head. We want to get it off without any more of the powder coming in contact with your skin if we can."

Comprehension finally overtook his bewilderment. He slammed his eyes shut, and she carefully lifted the shirt over his head. He stood stock-still, barely breathing and waiting for her next command.

"Okay," she murmured, and he wasn't sure if she was talking to him or to herself.

Cracking one eyelid, he peered at her through his lashes. "Okay what?"

"Shorts off," she said brusquely.

He opened his eyes to find her folding the shirt in on itself. Tucking his chin to his chest, Harry looked down and saw white streaks flowing down the front of his gym shorts. He hooked his thumbs into the waistband and then cautiously pulled the elastic away from his body so he could lower them to the tops of his shoes without the fabric turning inside out.

Alicia nodded her approval and offered her arm to him. "Steady yourself and step out of them. Then toe out of your shoes. Try not to disturb the stuff on the floor any more than you have to."

Harry did as she instructed, leaving the shorts in the pool on the floor and his running shoes a step behind them. He stood clad only in his boxer briefs and a pair of no-show socks, but before he could start to feel self-conscious about his seminudity, he realized the woman collecting the clothing possibly covered in a toxic substance also happened to be carrying his child.

Allegedly.

His gaze fell to the shirt she held clutched in one hand. "Hey, you need to drop the shirt," he told her.

Alicia looked up, lines of puzzlement bisecting her arched brows. "What? No. I have to preserve the scene if I can." She looked down at the sheets of paper scattered around them like debris from an explosion. "Step out of the area and head straight for the shower. Soap and water, nothing more," she ordered briskly. "Wash everything. Your hair, under your nails, everything. Lather, rinse, repeat. A few times if necessary. I'll call Ben Kinsella."

At the mention of the sheriff's name, Harry jolted. Reality came crashing into this bizarre daydream. He hadn't fully registered what was happening, but now he got it.

"You're pregnant," he murmured under his breath.

"We'll talk about it later. Right now, you need to go hit the shower."

He nodded dumbly. "Okay. Call Ben, but you need to put those things down and go wash up too. I mean it." Feeling better having gotten some of his own orders in, he slowly stepped out of the field of debris.

Alicia placed his folded shirt atop his shoes and stepped away. "I'll be fine. It didn't get any on me."

"You still breathed it in," he shot back. "And you touched my shirt. You should trash those gloves and wash your hands right away," he said with an emphatic nod. "There's a guest bath in the hallway. You go wash everything too."

"I'm fine."

"But you've been touching me," he pointed out. Harry gestured to the corridor leading to his bedroom at the end of the hall. "I'm going to the shower, but please at least go wash up." He jerked back, recalling the most salient point of the conversation they'd been having when the evening became even more surreal than he could possibly imagine.

"You're pregnant."

"Right." She nodded once, then looked down at her glove-covered hands. "I'll wash up, then call Ben. You get to the shower."

He did as he was told, because holy hell, what was it? Anthrax? Ricin? Rounding the corner into the master bath, Harry had to resist the urge to wet his now parched lips. He'd seen and heard enough about threats made on prosecutors. They weren't always empty. No matter how tempting it was, he couldn't risk it.

He didn't wait for the water to warm. He simply turned on the spray and stepped in, boxer briefs and all. He blindly washed his face three times before he dared to lick the shower's spray from his lips. Then he scrubbed his entire body from head to toe. Twice. On the third pass, he let his mind off the leash.

Alicia Simmons was in his living room. Alicia Simmons was pregnant. Alicia Simmons believed her baby was his. His baby.

But how?

The question was ludicrous on the surface, but it kept circling around in his brain. They hadn't gotten carried away in the back of a car like teenagers turned loose on a summer night. Okay, so they hadn't used a condom. Not the most responsible decision he'd ever made, but they'd talked. Frankly. Openly. Like adults. There had been informed consent. Both his and hers. A serious discussion about sexual health and birth control. She'd said she was on the pill. Tequila or not, he remembered one vital bit of information clearly. But there was only one truly foolproof form of birth control, and abstinence hadn't even seemed like an option at the time.

Switching off the water, Harry stood in his shower dazed and dripping. And somehow, he was still wearing his underwear. Scowling, he shucked off the soap-soaked briefs, turned the water back to full blast for a quick rinse, then twisted the knobs again. He shivered slightly when the water running from his shower head slowed to a rhythmic drip.

Placing both hands flat on the smooth tile, he hung his head and took three slow breaths to steady himself. White powder in an envelope. Slashed tires. Obscenities etched into his car doors with a key or other metal object. He shouldn't be shocked. These things happened when a person was prosecuting someone with a following. Heck, the vehicular vandalism wasn't a first for him. Of course, he hadn't been driving a new German-made sports sedan at the time. And his previously impugned Chevy had been considerably older than the tiny new model he'd driven home a scant four months ago. He hadn't cracked the spine on the owner's manual, and the new-car smell still lingered.

"She was only a baby," he murmured on a heavy sigh.

The last word lingered on his lips. Straightening his spine, he shook his wet hair back from his face. He opened the glass door wide enough to snare a towel from the bar and quickly wrapped it around his waist. Still dripping, he padded from the bathroom into his darkened bedroom. Light spilled down the hall. The low hum of hushed conversation drifted back to him.

Part of him wanted to rush out there. He needed to check on Alicia. Find out if they could tell exactly what the powdery substance was once the shock of it had worn off. But he needed clothes first.

After closing his bedroom door, he let the towel come loose as he strode to his closet. He ran the damp terry cloth over his head, then used it to dry himself from head to toe. Pulling a fresh pair of briefs from his dresser, he set to work putting his thoughts in order while he dressed.

These types of threats rarely involved actual toxins. Logically, he was aware it was likely a hoax. But there was always the chance. Besides, logic and statistics were standing firmly outside his circle of trust. He yanked a T-shirt from another drawer and shrugged into it. Sure, logic and statistical analysis might give him some comfort in regard to the contents of the package, but they failed when it came to calculating the probability of Alicia Simmons showing up at his house out of the blue to tell him he was about to become someone's daddy. Stepping into a pair of clean jeans, he hiked them over his hips and fastened them. He decided to forgo socks and shoes in favor of getting a few answers.

When he reached the end of the hall, he found

Deputy Lori Cabrera crouched over the scattered papers and holding up the torn envelope with a pair of long tweezers. She wore gloves and a disposable respirator mask. So did Sheriff Ben Kinsella, who stood next to his deputy holding a plastic evidence bag open wide.

"Hey." He spoke the greeting softly, not wanting to startle them in the midst of their work.

Lori looked up, her big brown eyes warm and reassuring. "Pretty sure we have a cornstarch situation."

Her words were slightly muffled by the mask, but he read her loud and clear. They'd still have to get the substance tested, though, which was the real damage done. Not only was it costing the sheriff and his deputy their time, but the crime lab would have to analyze the powder, the envelope and all the contents for proper identification and clues as to who might have sent it.

"No postage," Lori reported. "Someone hand delivered these season's greetings."

Great. Whoever had done this had dropped their package of doom directly on his front doorstep. "Anything in the papers?" he asked, hopeful, but not expecting much.

To his surprise, Ben nodded. "Actually, yes."

He gestured to the pile, and Lori raised one of the sheets of paper. Someone had drawn a picture in pencil but carefully erased it. The lines were faint, though he could make out the crude rendering of a coiled snake with the words Don't Tread on Me printed beneath it.

"Oh, well, no points for subtlety," Harry said as he ran his hand over his face, suddenly drained.

"No," a husky voice agreed from behind him.

Harry jumped and turned to find Alicia standing in the kitchen area. There was dark amusement in her tone. In truth, her wry cynicism was what had drawn him to her two months before. Now it rankled. Someone had left an envelope addressed to him and filled with mysterious powder at his front door. Cornstarch or not, this was getting out of hand.

"Step back." Ben shooed Harry toward the kitchen, then opened more evidence bags. Lori steadily and methodically worked her way through the papers, bagging each one individually in hopes the lab might be able to lift a print or two. "So, we're assuming this is related to Samuel Coulter's case," the sheriff said gruffly. "Anything else happening? Any new developments?"

Biting the inside of his cheek, he cast a sidelong glance at Alicia. He wasn't too keen on the idea of spelling out all the mini- and macroaggressions he'd suffered since Samuel Coulter and some of his compatriots were brought up on charges of drug and human trafficking, but it wasn't like she wouldn't hear about it all eventually. This would be one topic of conversation among many, he figured.

He shrugged, trying to play it cool, but one of the threats had made it into his house. He felt shakier than he cared to admit. "The usual. Threatening calls. Callouts on social media. Some minor vandalism."

Ben's eyes narrowed. "I saw your car. They scrape it up here or at the office?"

Harry raised his brows, a sardonic smile tugging at the corner of his mouth. "You mean here or four blocks away from here?" Beside him, Alicia snickered softly. He was embarrassed to admit how much he liked hearing it. "It happened here."

Alicia pivoted then. "Someone damaged your car?"

"Punctured a couple tires one night, keyed the paint job another," he reported, his tone dispassionate. Turning his attention back to Ben, he said, "Those incidents both happened here."

"So, it's someone who has your home address," Alicia mused.

Harry couldn't contain his bark of laughter. The same amusement danced in Lori's eyes before she refocused on her task. Only Ben refrained from showing how entertaining the question might be to anyone accustomed to small-town life.

"Most everyone in town knows where he lives," Ben explained. Harry couldn't determine if the note of apology he detected in his friend's tone was because he was tuned in to how ridiculous life in a town like Pine Bluff could be, or because he was a onetime city dweller with an urbanite's casual assumption of anonymity. "This town is pretty small, and Harry is the sucker who gives the kids the big candy bars at Halloween."

He shrugged again. "Someone has to do it."

Beside him, Alicia hummed her disapproval. "I'm surprised you're not more careful. There's always a chance someone looking for some payback might search you out."

For the first time since he'd opened the door to find her standing on his welcome mat, it occurred to Harry she must have done the same—searched him out. After all, they hadn't come back to his place when they left Simon's party. No, they'd gone to the rental house she'd lived in for less than a month. But somehow, she had found him.

"How'd you get my address?"

"Why don't you park in your garage?" she asked simultaneously.

Time stood still for a second. Somewhere, in the back of his mind, he couldn't help thinking two people who were having a child together should have the answers to these types of questions. But they didn't. They were virtual strangers who'd come together high on victory and drunk on tequila.

"I, uh, I use the garage as a gym," he said at last.

"Ben gave up the goods on your address," she admitted, shooting her friend an apologetic glance. "But it's not his fault. I told him I wanted to send you a Christmas card."

"A Christmas card," he repeated blankly.

She smirked. "Seemed a good excuse."

Harry went on high alert the moment Ben Kinsella turned his flat cop stare on him. "I guess she decided to deliver your card in person, Harry."

"None of your business, boss," Lori murmured, scooping white powder into vials to be sent into the crime lab. Harry let out a gusty breath when Ben swung his glare toward his insubordinate deputy. But Lori returned it, unperturbed. "Unless you think our friendly DEA agent was the one to send our district attorney an envelope full of fake anthrax."

Alicia laughed, and Ben's stony expression softened. "No, I feel pretty confident Alicia sends her messages more directly."

"You've got that right," the woman in question replied, unfazed by the turn the conversation had taken. "I am here because I wanted to talk to Harry about some things."

Ben's cop face returned with a vengeance. "Things I need to be aware of?" he asked, his tone sharpening.

Alicia shook her head. "No. If they were, I would have come to you. This was information specifically for Mr. Hayes."

For one minute, Harry was afraid she might blurt out her reason for being there. Thankfully, Deputy Cabrera rescued him.

"There. I think we have enough."

Harry eyed the dusting of powder coating his living-room floor. "And you're sure it wasn't anything dangerous?"

"We're sure," the three answered in almost perfect unison.

They chuckled, and Harry was forced to crack a smile at last. "Okay, well, all right." He clapped his hands together. "I guess I should break out the old Shop-Vac."

Ben nodded, then pulled an individually wrapped mask and gloves from the kit Lori was repacking. "Here. To be on the safe side," he said, thrusting the personal protective equipment at Harry.

"And poof! My warm fuzzy feeling is gone," Harry grumbled.

Chapter Three

The moment Harry closed the door behind Ben and Lori, Alicia's nerves rushed to the surface of her skin. She stood in the kitchen doorway, feeling twitchy as a teenager on her first date. But she was way beyond her teenage awkwardness. She and Harry may not have ever had a first date, but they had a baby coming. And someone was threatening him.

God, what a night.

Harry stood in the foyer, his hands braced on his hips and his head bowed. His posture made him appear both thoughtful and vulnerable. A quality she recognized as one of the reasons she'd been so attracted to him to start. He was confident, but not cocksure. A potently powerful combination.

And his winning vulnerability made her ache to reassure him.

"Harry, I don't want to mess up your life," she said, injecting an abundance of sincerity into the sentiment. "I'm a grown woman. I have a good job, and I can take care of myself and this baby. I didn't come here expecting you to upend everything you've built for yourself because we got reckless one night."

"Reckless," he repeated softly.

"But you see, the odds of this baby ever happening were so microscopically slim…" She trailed off with a laugh. "I have a complicated medical history, and this might be my one and only chance. And while I think I'm ready to grab hold of it, I want you to understand I absolutely do not expect you to alter any of your plans for the present or future."

He lifted his head at last. "Then why come here to tell me?"

There was no accusation in the question. He asked purely out of curiosity. Unfortunately, she didn't have a truly satisfactory answer. She had no idea why it had seemed so important to tell him. She could've gone on with her life and he never would've been the wiser. But doing so felt dishonest. She didn't want to make her baby a secret. Treat her child as something to be ashamed of. And the last thing Alicia wanted was for this baby to come into a world doubting they were wanted wholeheartedly.

"Would you have rather I made it a secret?" she asked, needing reassurance she'd done the right thing. "I thought no, but maybe I was wrong. Was I wrong?"

His hands fell away from his hips, and he raised one to scrub his face and smooth his hair back into place. "No, you weren't wrong."

He stated his position with such clarity, she

couldn't help but smile with relief. "Listen, this night has been, well, a lot," she said with a laugh. "Let's take some time and maybe talk again in a day or two?"

He eyed her carefully for a moment, then nodded. "Probably a good idea."

"I'll leave you all of my contact information," she offered. "You can use it or not. No hard feelings either way."

"No hard feelings," he echoed, his tone hushed with disbelief.

"I mean it. I meant it when I said I could handle this on my own. I can, and I will. Actually, going it alone was my intention all along. My coming here was more of a...courtesy." She stepped out of the kitchen and into the open-plan living area. The place was still an utter mess. "Would you like me to help you clean up?"

He shook his head. "I've got this."

Her mind played back the discussion he and Ben had about the damages done to his car. "Do you often get threats against you?"

He cocked his head and it was clear from his expression he considered her question slightly ridiculous. "I'm a prosecutor. People are seldom happy when I bring charges against them. Even more unhappy if I win. And even if they go to jail, those people often have family members who are happy to carry their unhappiness for them." He shrugged. "This is all part of the territory."

"But do they usually strike so close to home? Literally," she said, gesturing to the mess on the floor.

He didn't bother trying to deny it. Instead, he shook his head and cast a mournful gaze at his dust-covered floor. "No, not this close."

"Coulter has friends. He has some unsavory friends," she said pointedly.

"I'm aware."

"If this gets to be too much, if this escalates in any way, you need to ask for protection."

"Protection," he said with a soft snort. "If we were going to pick a word of the night, right?"

Alicia couldn't stifle her laugh. Gallows humor was often the refuge of law enforcement, and it appeared their counterparts on the judiciary side of things were no different. "In both cases, I think the horse is out of the barn, but you can take steps to protect yourself."

"I'll take your recommendation under advisement," he said dryly. Alicia watched him draw a deep breath in and then let it out slowly. At last, he took a step closer to her and looked her in the eye. "Are you planning to drive back to Atlanta tonight?"

She nodded. "I planned on it. Why?"

"I'm not sure." He rolled his shoulders back and torqued his head to the side to stretch his neck. "It's late," he said.

Alicia glanced down at the sports watch strapped to her wrist. "It's seven twenty-two."

"I mean, it's dark…and cold…" He trailed off. "You're traveling alone."

"I often do," she said briskly. "Again, I'm a grown woman. I can take care of myself. And if anyone tries to mess with me, I have a gun, remember?"

He reared back. "On you? I've never seen you carry."

"That's because I don't wave my gun around. It's either in a holster or in my bag. Tonight, it's in my bag," she said, lifting her brows and fixing him with a pointed stare. "Would you like to see my concealed carry permit?"

"No." He shook his head, then had the good grace to laugh at himself. "I never thought of you carrying a weapon. Every time I've seen you, you've been more on the command side of things, I guess. I thought you were a suit. Like me," he added with a winsome smile.

"I am," she said, amused. "But I'm also armed at all times. The suit helps cover the holster."

He chuckled and shook his head, running a hand over his mouth, a hint of color touching his cheeks and the tips of his ears. "I'm not sure if I should be terrified or turned on," he admitted.

"I recommend both," she answered without hesitation.

"Sorry, I didn't mean to imply you were any less of an agent because…" He shot her a look from under his lashes. "It never occurred to me."

"It's because I'm so feminine," she said with an edge of sarcasm.

His brow crinkled. He was working hard to determine if she were joking or not. "You are."

She snickered. "Don't fret, Counselor. I'm not going to shoot you."

He looked up into her eyes and his gaze never wavered. He studied her, searching for a clue as to whether he'd stuck his foot in some kind of a trap. "But you are. Feminine, I mean. From where I've stood, you always have been. Both strong and feminine," he said with a decisive nod.

Alicia was so disarmed by his mild stammering, she decided to let him off the hook easy. "Thank you. I am. I never could understand why some men think a woman can't own her sexuality as well as a SIG Sauer."

This time, he let out a full-blown laugh. Country raised, he couldn't help appreciating a woman who was more comfortable talking about handguns than handbags. "Okay, now you are definitely trying to turn me on," he accused.

Alicia felt her own cheeks warm with a flush of pleasure. On impulse, she reached for his hand and gave it a squeeze. She would not think about how good those hands had felt on her. She had more important matters to focus on now. A baby. Her baby.

"I'll go to the doctor to get things verified. The due date will be pretty easy to calculate, since there's no wondering about the date of conception…" She snapped her mouth shut and inhaled deeply through her nose. Once she felt more in control, she gave him a wan smile. "I should have more information by the end of the week."

Reaching into her bag, she pulled out one of the business cards she kept loose in an inside pocket. "I never got a chance to give you this before I left Pine Bluff, but here's all my contact info."

He scissored the proffered card between his fore and middle fingers but made no move to pull it from her grasp. "Would you have?"

His voice was rough. Gravelly with exhaustion and emotion. She recognized it from the long hours they'd spent working together to make sure he had every scrap of evidence he needed to bring Coulter in front of a judge and ask that the millionaire be held without bail because he was a flight risk. A federal prosecutor had been assigned to the case, but Alicia convinced him to take Harrison as his second chair. Since he'd been born and raised in Masters County, she'd thought Harry might hold more sway with a jury in rural Georgia. But then Coulter had thrown them all for a loop by waiving his right to trial by jury. Now Harry was a hanger-on in a case scheduled to be heard by a federal judge in another town, but receiving threats from the slimebags who lived in his own backwoods.

"I'd planned to, but then you got busy and I got busy and we never, uh…"

"Got busy again?" he supplied, taking the card from her at last.

She nodded. "Yeah." She hiked the strap of her bag up on her shoulder. "Then I got a call saying I was needed back in Atlanta, and, well, I guess it felt awkward," she confessed.

To her relief, he nodded. "I get you."

"But the card has all my numbers plus an email address." She indicated the card. "You don't have to use them if you don't want to." She raised both hands to ward him off. "If you want to be a part of this baby's life, I will do everything in my power to make it happen, but if you choose not to be, no judgment. The only thing I ask is you take some time to think it over before you decide."

He nodded, but she had to press on with the hard part before he got too agreeable.

"Harry, I need you to be certain. If you opt out, I will ask you to relinquish all rights. Not to be spiteful, but because I don't want to leave things open to chaos and confusion later. Do you understand where I'm coming from?"

"Yeah," he croaked.

"Take your time, okay?" She smiled and gave her still-flat stomach a pat. "It's a big decision, but we have time to figure it all out."

"Right." He cleared his throat, then nodded more emphatically, dragging his gaze from her hand. "Definitely. Yes. Not something to make rash decisions about, for sure."

They stood there, eyeing each other, waiting for the other to make the first move. Never one to shy away from diving in, Alicia gave him a quick nod, let her hand fall away from her belly, then stepped toward the door.

"Wait," Harry blurted, reaching out to take hold of her arm.

Alicia instinctively looked down at his hand before lifting her gaze to his. The moment their eyes met, he released his hold. "Yes?" she asked, tamping down the flicker of hope flaring where their baby nestled in her womb.

"Have you eaten?"

The question was so far from her train of thought it might have parachuted in from a plane. "What?"

"Dinner. Have you eaten?" he asked again, his tone slightly more persistent.

She shook her head. "No, I haven't, but I'm not sure I will," she said with a grimace.

"You need to eat," he insisted. "Because you're pregnant."

She gave a soft laugh, tipping her head to the side as if conceding his point, then shaking it firmly. "This isn't a good time for me."

"Not a good time? Are you in a hurry or something?" he asked, a note of irritability creeping into his tone. "Anxious to drop your bombs and fly off into the rising sun or something?"

"Rising sun?"

"Tactical maneuver. Blinds people trying to take you out with antiaircraft fire," he said with a shrug.

"Are you former air force or something?"

"Or something," he replied. When she let the silence stretch, he huffed out a breath. "I like war movies, video games and stuff," he said with a dismissive wave of his hand.

"Ah," she breathed. "A nerd."

He narrowed his eyes. "I appreciate a strategic assault. Like to employ them too."

"Do you now?"

"Some people use weapons—I use words." He crossed his arms over his chest. "Coulter and his new attorneys think a bench trial will get a good chunk of the evidence against him thrown out on technicalities. They're banking on not needing to appeal to a jury. They want to slip through loopholes in the letters of the law."

"Do you think he can?"

Harry exhaled long and loud, turning away. "Maybe. He'll wriggle out of at least some of them. Like you're trying to wriggle out of sitting down to eat a meal with me."

"I'm not…" She started and stopped, not sure why she was trying to play it coy all of a sudden when she'd come through this man's front door with a proverbial battering ram. "I, uh… Morning sickness is a misnomer," she finally said.

"Excuse me?"

"I don't get sick in the morning. Or as sick, I

should say. It's morning, noon and night sickness for me, but it seems to hit me harder at night," she explained, lifting her chin a notch, practically daring him to tell her she and her body were being ridiculous with their refusal to follow the rules.

His face went blank for a second. Then realization dawned. "Oh."

"So, yeah, I've mostly been eating crackers at night. I thought it was a stomach bug at first, but then the smell of soup set me off. A colleague's wife was the same way. I remembered her, and it made me think maybe…" She gave him a shaky smile.

"I can make something easy, like some plain pasta," he offered.

"You're sweet, but I think we both may need those couple days," she said gently. "This is new for me too, and though I am sure I want this baby, I haven't had much time to process it."

Again, he scraped a hand over his face. "You're not going to…disappear again, right?"

"I gave you all my contact information," she reminded him.

"Calls can go unanswered, and emails can be trashed. And something tells me I'm not going to be able to score your home address by saying I want to send a Christmas card."

Her smile widened. "I think I've already blown my chance at remaining a woman of mystery. Plus, I came here to tell you, didn't I?"

"Promise you're not dropping this bomb and heading for the horizon," he persisted. "This whole night has been beyond wild. I need you to give me your word we will talk again."

Alicia sobered in an instant. "I give you my word."

He nodded in concession. "Can I give you anything for the drive back? Water? I don't have any fancy crackers, but I think I have some saltines. You did say you can eat crackers, right?"

"Right. And yes. A bottle of water and some saltines would be great," she said, sensing it would give him comfort and provide her with something to settle her rebellious stomach.

Harry nodded. "Be right back."

She moved toward the door, her hand hooked around the strap of her bag, but her gaze strayed to the streaks of powder trailing into the hall. Guilt twinged in her gut. If she hadn't picked the stupid envelope up and brought it inside, some richly deserving porch pirate might have swiped it and gotten a poof in the face and an hour of panic for their perfidy.

"You're sure you don't want help cleaning up?" she called toward the back of the house.

"No, I'm good." Harry reappeared, a plastic grocery sack dangling from his fingers. "I had some electrolyte water. It might help. I threw it in with a couple bottles of regular water. And the crackers, of course."

Alicia accepted the offering, a smile tugging at the corners of her mouth when she spotted an entire box of saltines nestled in with three large bottles of water. "It's only a little over three hours' drive." She let the grin grow. His hazel gaze was sincere. "If I drink all this, it'll be over four hours with stops."

Harry rolled his eyes. "Sip, don't guzzle."

He moved past her to open the front door. She stood there a moment, taking in the sight of his handsome face bathed in the warm light. The night beyond him was dark and still. The breeze had died down, but the air was now crisp and cool. Beyond his front porch, the citizens of Pine Bluff were all nestled in for a long winter's evening of television and other indoor activities.

She was about to say something insane about what a pretty street he lived on when she heard a sharp crack and saw a puff of brick and mortar explode beside his head. Alicia dropped the bag and grabbed the front of his jeans—the first handhold she could get on him—and yanked him down to the floor.

Rolling her body on top of his, she flailed a foot out to kick the door closed. The heavy oak swung shut on well-oiled hinges. The moment of breathless suspension was shattered by the crack of another shot. Through the glass pane set in the top of the door, they watched as Harrison's porch light exploded in a shower of sparks.

Chapter Four

Gunfire. Someone was shooting at his house. They were under fire. And he was under Alicia.

Alicia Simmons was covering his body with hers while one of the unhinged hillbillies he'd dealt with his entire life took potshots at his house. Again.

Alicia thought she was saving him. She thought she was saving him by dragging him down to the floor and covering his body with hers. Her much smaller body. Her pregnant body.

The second the thought popped into his head, his body reacted. Hooking his leg over both of hers, he wrapped his arms tight around her and rolled until their positions were reversed.

"What are you doing?" she asked, breathless.

"What do you think you're doing?" he panted back.

"There's someone shooting at the house."

No sooner were the words out of her mouth than a rain of pellets sprayed the house and the narrow pane of glass beside his front door splintered into a spiderweb of cracks.

"What the hell?" Alicia huffed, straining to look toward the door. "Get off me."

"No." He backed his refusal with action. Digging his bare toes into the floor, he slid them about three feet away from the door.

"Damn it, Harry, someone is shooting at your house."

Beneath him, she wriggled and squirmed, and at one point balled up her fist and struck his shoulder. He shook his head, and she retracted her arm again. Thankfully, she telegraphed her punch by staring too hard at his jaw. He ducked his head at the last second and her knuckles glanced off the side of his skull.

"Ow! Damn it, Harry, let me up."

"Not on your life," he muttered.

His foot brushed something solid, and he looked back to see it was her purse. Flexing his foot, he caught the bulk of the bag and scooted it toward his outstretched hand. He could feel her body coil and tensed for another blow. "Hang on a sec," he ordered. "I have your purse."

"Good," she huffed. "I need my gun."

Harrison felt his eyebrows shoot up, but as he groped around in the soft leather bag, he hoped he didn't grab hold of a firearm. The moron spraying the front of his house with birdshot wasn't looking for a firefight. They only wanted to get his attention. A gun was the last thing they needed, but he didn't trust himself not to fire back if the weapon fell into his hand.

He stilled for a moment, listening closely. No more shots fired. Whoever it was had probably run for the woods. Probably feeling triumphant. After all, they'd taken out a perfectly good porch light and a whole window. He was shaking with rage when, thankfully, his hand closed around her cell phone.

"Here," he said, shoving the instrument into her flailing hand. "Call Ben. Tell him someone is using the house for target practice again."

"Again?"

He looked down to find her staring up at him, her eyes wide with alarm. Nodding, he said, "I'm guessing buckshot this time. Someone used birdshot before, and it didn't do much more than mess up the paint on the porch."

To his relief, he saw her thumbing the screen. "Does this happen often?"

He heard the quaver in her voice, and something in him unraveled. "No, not often," he assured her. "It's just…there's been some trouble. I won another motion today. It's not unusual for tensions to escalate as we get closer to opening arguments. People don't need much of an excuse to get riled these days, and Coulter has kicked over more than a few dead logs around here."

"You weigh a ton. Get off me," she complained, but then Ben must have picked up because she jerked her attention to the call. "No. Uh, not you, Ben. Listen, someone is shooting at Hayes's house." She listened for a moment, her face slackening in incredulity before she rolled her eyes. "Yes, again. He says to tell you it looks like buckshot this time, but I'm pretty sure something higher caliber took out the porch light," she said, sliding a pointed glare at Harry. "The first two shots were rifle fire."

He pressed up on his hands, relieving her of some of his weight, but not enough for her to slip out from under him and start running down the street with her gun in hand. To make her feel better, he conceded her point with a nod. "Could have been more than one of them. These guys rarely fly solo on missions."

Alicia's forehead puckered as she listened to Ben issuing opinions and instructions. "Okay. Yeah. Okay, I'll stick." She ended the call and met Harry's eyes again. "He said you're probably right—he's going to cruise out to somebody called Arnie Smithson's place, and I'm to hang here until he calls back."

"Good idea." Pressing into a full push-up, Harry lifted a hand and flipped over off her. Alicia immediately scuttled into a sitting position, but he had trapped her handbag behind him against the foyer wall. "No need for the gun," he informed her, his voice calmer than he felt in his gut.

She glowered at him as she crossed her legs like a kindergartner and pushed her hair away from her face. "I am a trained law enforcement officer," she reminded him.

"I'm aware. You also just told me you're pregnant," he retorted a shade too sharply.

"It's not a disability. I can still do my job," she shot back.

He raised both hands in surrender. "I'm only saying you might try to remember the change in status the next time you throw someone to the floor and cover them with your own body."

Her cheeks flushed a pretty pink, but Harry refused to be drawn in by it. At least, he did his best not to. Lord, she looked beautiful with the color riding high on her cheekbones and her eyes gleaming with determination.

"I could always use the whole 'My body, my decision' argument."

He narrowed his eyes. "It was your decision to come here and make sure I was aware of what was happening with your body."

"But I didn't give you a say," she countered.

He leveled his most stern "speaking directly to one juror" stare on her. "I'm asking you, please do not do anything to place you or your baby in harm's way on my behalf."

She seemed to sag, the fight seeping out of her bones. For the first time since she'd stepped through the door, he noticed how tired she looked. Dark smudges under her eyes. Her skin pasty under all her bluster. The starch in her spine softened and all traces of defensiveness disappeared. Maybe because he referred to the child she was carrying in the singular possessive? He wasn't sure. As long as it kept her from charging out his front door and into the night, he didn't care.

"There are some groups of people who go looking for trouble," he said quietly. "They're loosely organized gangs of thugs, but Ben refers to them as militia. Coulter made friends with a couple of them, and now they feel the need to take up the fight for him."

"Oh."

The single syllable slipped out of her on a whisper, but it spoke volumes in understanding. He nodded, confirming every scenario he feared might be running through her head. Ben had clued in to the big picture fast enough when things started getting personal in the past few weeks. But the fact that the envelope had been dropped on his doorstep on the same night someone else decided to do some target shooting disturbed him.

The thugs Arnie Smithson ran with were not the brightest bulbs, but they were savvy enough to spread their mischief out over a stretch of time. Make it last. Rotate perpetrators so no single person could be brought in on multiple charges. Harry and Ben understood what many city slickers failed to grasp. The people they were dealing with might be uneducated and uncouth, but they were far from stupid.

"Ben is a good cop. We need to sit tight and let him do his job."

Not surprisingly, Alicia reached into her bag again and came up with her gun and a slim leather ID case. "It's my job too," she said, lifting a challenging eyebrow.

He wasn't entirely certain if he wanted to hug her or shake her. Instead, he stared her down, though it took almost every ounce of energy he had not to reach for her.

"Listen, Dirty Harriett, unless you spotted someone doing a deal on my front doorstep, you have no jurisdiction here." He extended the first two fingers of his right hand and pushed the barrel of her firearm to the side. "I have more right to discharge a weapon on these premises than you do."

To his relief, the corner of her mouth lifted in a smirk. "Dirty Harriett? You need to get some movie references from this century...Harry."

Her pointed emphasis of his name made him smile in return. "You understood the reference," he retorted.

To his relief, Alicia shoved her weapon and credentials back into her bag. "Do you keep a .44 Magnum handy, in case some punk feels lucky?"

"No, but I have my granddad's old .22 for when I want to put the fear of God into a few squirrels."

"You hunt squirrels?" she asked, wrinkling her nose. "I thought you said you didn't like hunting."

He found the girlish reaction oddly enchanting. She was such a straightforward, capable woman. It was funny to think of her getting grossed out by anything. "I haven't since my granddad passed, but

I think I can manage to defend the homestead if the need arises."

"How do you defend against stuff like this?" she asked, her voice rising with exasperation as she gestured toward the front porch.

"By putting bad guys behind bars," he replied without missing a beat. At her skeptical snort, he shrugged. "Those yahoos are simply looking for something to get riled about. The Coulter case—and me by extension—is their flavor of the week. Don't worry. They're bound to latch on to whatever is the latest conspiracy theory coming out of news talk radio, and by next week they'll have forgotten all about me."

"The blessings of the twenty-four-hour news cycle," she said dryly. "I don't see how you can stand it."

"Stand what?"

"Living out here with all these rebels," she said derisively.

"You forget—I am one of these people." He crossed his arms over his chest.

She snorted. "Hardly."

"I went to school with Andy Smithson, Arnie's younger brother. I was born here. These people have been my neighbors my whole life."

Alicia exhaled long and loud, but her gaze never wavered. "Hard to believe. Anyhow, yes, Counselor, unless I'm in a bathing suit, you can believe I'm carrying. Even then, I probably have a gun in my beach bag."

He shrugged, then nodded to her purse. "I'm afraid to ask what else you have in there."

Her hair swung forward, partially shielding her face as she opened the purse wide for his perusal, then rummaged around in its cavernous depths. "Nothing unusual. Lipstick tubes, a Glock, a compact, my wallet, zip-tie cuffs, phone charger, granola bar, cond…" Her voice trailed away, and the last syllable hung there unspoken.

A beat passed. Then he ran his hand through his hair with a harsh choke of laughter. "Sure, now you have protection."

"I bought them at the pharmacy downtown, uh, the morning after," she said quietly. "I didn't want to get caught without again."

He swallowed hard, a thousand unanswered questions bubbling up inside him, fighting to burst out. But he kept the lid clamped tightly. He swooped down and snagged the handles of the plastic bag he'd given her mere minutes before. Gesturing to the kitchen, he said, "Come back in and sit down. It's going to be a bit until Ben sounds the all clear, and we need to talk."

Seated at his kitchen table with bottles of water and a package of saltines open in front of Alicia, he asked the one question swirling in his mind. "How do you think this happened? And not the technical stuff. I mean, we discussed birth control…"

She nibbled a bit of cracker but didn't drop his gaze. "I cut my finger slicing lemons. I didn't think much about it, but a couple days later I noticed it was red and tender. I had an infection, so the doctor gave me antibiotics. I was taking them when I came down here."

Her pointed stare told him she thought she'd imparted sufficient explanation, but for the life of him, Harry was having a hard time connecting the dots. Tired of trying to figure things out, he made a motion for her to continue.

"Antibiotics can sometimes impact the efficacy of birth control pills," she explained, her delivery flat. "It's usually recommended people use some form of backup contraceptive—"

"Like a condom," he interjected.

She inclined her head. "Like a condom," she conceded, "if they plan to have intercourse."

"I see."

"I didn't plan to have intercourse, nor was I overly worried about the birth control failing because I have a condition… It makes my chances of conception lower than average," she said, opening her hands in a helpless motion.

"You mentioned something about a complicated medical background," he prompted. "What condition?"

"Yes, well…" She paused. "It's called polycystic ovarian syndrome, but it's kind of a moot point now, isn't it? I'm pregnant, so what I thought couldn't happen, or at least wouldn't happen easily, has actually, uh, occurred."

She ducked her head for the first time, and all of a sudden, Harry was struck by how much it must have cost her to come here and tell him this news. She could have kept her secret, and he would never have been the wiser. Would being oblivious have been better or worse? He wasn't sure.

"I swear I would never have done something like this intentionally. I mean, you remember the whole discussion we had about consent, right?"

Remember it? He still chuckled each time he thought about it. She'd been the initiator. At first. But the minute he'd caught up with her seduction and thrown himself into the action, she'd pulled back. She'd pulled back and spelled out what was about to happen between them in no uncertain terms. Then, unsatisfied with his eager nodding, she'd demanded verbal assent. They'd gone through the same routine again when they realized they didn't have a condom close at hand, with the addition of a curt briefing on medical and sexual history.

As though she could read his thoughts, Alicia spoke. "It was an accident, Harry. It sounds lame, but it's the truth." She reached across the table and gave his hand a squeeze. "It's a shock. I get it. Truthfully, it is for me too, but it's a happy accident for me. It may not be for you, and I understand." She closed her eyes as if mustering the strength to speak words she wasn't entirely certain she could. "In truth, happy or not, my head is in a whirl. I have no idea what I'm going to do." She gave him a wry smile.

"I only want you to believe me when I say I have no intention of trying to derail your life. You may want nothing to do with this child once it's born, and no matter what, I will respect your choices."

"How could you think I'd want nothing to do with my own child?" The words were out of his mouth before he'd even had time to process them. And since he'd always been a man to go with his gut reaction, Harry didn't quibble with himself. "Wait. No. I retract the question. Of course, you couldn't know how I would react. I wouldn't have guessed how I'd react," he said with a laugh.

"We don't know each other well at all." She gave his hand another squeeze and he looked down at their clasped fingers. "Except in the biblical sense."

He chuckled at her blunt assessment, then shook his head. "I wish I'd reacted better."

"I think we could both use some time to let this… unexpected turn of events settle." She gave him a shaky smile. "Probably not gonna happen tonight, though, right? We need time to be practical…think rationally about all aspects of what this can mean for both of us. And tonight isn't turning out to be a night for calm consideration."

This time, his laugh came easier. Pinching his temples, he rubbed his forehead. "It's been a doozy." Turning his hand over, he gave her fingers a warm squeeze in return. "Can we agree to table any further discussion until we've both had the opportunity to think things through?"

"Absolutely."

Alicia gently slipped her hand from his. Harry felt the loss of her warmth immediately. He lowered his hand to his lap and clenched it into a loose fist to keep from reaching for her again. "Would you consider spending the night? I mean, I have a guest room…"

"Oh, I'm not sure."

He understood her hesitation. She obviously hadn't come prepared to spend the night in Pine Bluff, but a small irrational part of him wanted to make sure she never opened his front door again. People using his house for target practice aside, the thought of watching her walk out the door and her driving back to Atlanta made him uneasy. Not because he didn't think she was fully capable of making it home safely. He had too much confidence in her capabilities.

She'd done what she thought was the right thing by telling him about her condition. But now he had been informed, and she could decide to go back to Atlanta and her life there without giving him a chance to determine how he might fit into her new reality.

"Stay tonight," he said gruffly. "I'll pull out a frozen pizza, and you can have the crackers, and we can spend some time getting better acquainted—in a non-biblical way, I mean."

Alicia eyed him with wary skepticism. "Thank

you for the offer," she began. "But I'm not sure it's a good idea."

An odd sensation slithered through him, leaving him feeling inexplicably bereft. Unsure what else to do, he stepped back and lobbed a Hail Mary of an attempt at keeping her there. "Are you really going to leave me here all by myself with a bunch of crazies shooting at my house?"

Her eyebrows rose. "Are you really asking me to stay the night in the house under siege? You think it's better I stay here and risk being taken out by someone who thinks your house is a shooting arcade?"

Harrison couldn't help but laugh. When viewed from her position, his request sounded even more unreasonable. He understood. He was a man who weighed his options, calculated the odds and angled for the best possible outcome. All he could hope for here and now was to keep appealing to the same sense of ethics that brought her to his door. "Safety in numbers?"

"Speaking of safety," she said, then pressed her lips together as if she was fighting the urge to go on.

"Yes?"

"Have you considered taking a step back from the Coulter case?" She asked the question in such a rush, the words almost piled up on each other.

"No."

"I mean, it's not like you're the lead on it," she persisted. "But since you do live here locally, it's obviously more of a risk to you."

"Do you plan to?"

She blinked in surprise. "Do I plan to what?"

"You're slated to testify. You are the DEA's main witness. Tell me, do you plan to take a step back?"

The question wasn't exactly fair, but he couldn't help asking, if only to make his point. Clearly, she'd never considered walking away from the case. And if it weren't for the news she'd given him earlier, he never would have asked. But now…

"You're pregnant."

She sat up straighter. Harry could practically see her hackles rising. "So?"

He rolled his eyes at the lame comeback. "So, you're not only putting yourself in harm's way."

Her mouth tightened, but she didn't look away. If anything, her intense gaze burned brighter, likely fueled by the perceived challenge to her autonomy. Heaving a sigh, Harry dropped his voice and did his best to de-escalate the discussion. "Okay, not entirely fair, but there's more at stake today than there was even yesterday. I'd like us to be able to talk about this."

"I will testify at the trial. Nothing is going to change my mind," she retorted. "This is my case. Has been from the start."

"And I have been waiting for the chance to go after Coulter since the man moved to town," he replied, keeping his tone even. "But I'll back down if you will."

The offer made her flinch. "Are you saying you'd walk away from this case if I did?"

"It's not only about you or me anymore, is it?" he challenged.

"We're getting way ahead of ourselves," she said, waving his arguments off with wide swoops of her hands.

"We are," he agreed.

"I'll go back to Atlanta and set up an appointment to confirm everything. I'm going to need—" her voice tangled, but she pressed two fingers to her throat and carried on "—I'm going to figure out how I'll be handling things on my end. In the meantime, maybe we should refrain from making any hasty decisions."

"I think taking some time is a great idea." He fixed his gaze on her and held steady. "Promise me one thing."

"Okay," she agreed cautiously. "What?"

"Promise me you won't go back to Atlanta and never speak to me again," he said, his voice hoarse with churning uncertainty. "Promise me you're not going to drop this bombshell on my life and then disappear. If this is what's happening, I need to be…" He paused, searching for the correct word. "I need to be informed. I need to be able to make informed decisions, and I need you to respect me enough to let me be a part of those decisions."

"Harry," she said, staring straight into his eyes. "I came here."

"Right." He swallowed hard, then nodded as if by doing so he might convince himself. "Right."

Her phone lit up with an incoming call. Harry didn't need to check the display. It would be Ben on the line.

He listened with only half an ear as she took the call, speaking to the sheriff with the same economy of words cops seemed to pride themselves on. She ended the call, and Harry let his gaze follow as she rose from her seat.

"Ben's on his way back to take our statements. He said to tell you Arnie was home when he went by, and his wife… Annelle, is it?" she asked. When he nodded, she continued. "His wife and kids all swear he's been there all night. This Arnie guy also says he has no idea who might have shot up your house."

"Right. Of course he doesn't."

"Harry?"

"Yeah?"

"Would you mind if I took you up on the offer of your guest room? If we're going to do another round of statements, I'm not sure I'm going to be clear-headed enough to drive home after."

"I don't mind at all, as long as you don't mind if I go ahead with the pizza."

"Ugh, pizza." Alicia pushed the package of saltines aside and bolted from her chair.

When he heard the door to the guest bath close behind her, Harry winced. "So it's a no on the pizza."

He got up, snagged a jar of peanut butter from a cabinet and a knife from a drawer, and sat back down with the abandoned sleeve of saltines.

Chapter Five

"Thirty-eight?" Alicia repeated into the phone.

"According to the Southern Poverty Law Center's map as of last year," Ben Kinsella responded.

Alicia decided there was no better way to pass the early-morning drive from Pine Bluff to Atlanta than to pick the sheriff's brain about the rabble-rousers who inhabited Masters County.

"Of course, those are only the hate groups organized enough to be recognized," he continued.

"Right," she drawled.

"You can't be too surprised," he prodded. "The political climate around here is a tinderbox. People seem to be looking for a reason to be angry these days."

The truly sad part was, she was surprised, even though she shouldn't have been. Alicia was glad he couldn't see her slack-jawed expression through the phone. She made every effort she could to check her privileged status, but there were times when the truth about the world they lived in jumped up and slapped her. There were thirty-eight known, organized hate groups in the state of Georgia alone. Groups so active in promoting their particular brand of radicalized thinking they were kept on a watch list. They had no idea how many independent-minded vigilantes were hiding deep in the pine woods.

"You think some of them have adopted Coulter as their poster boy?" she asked.

"Oh, they have. Subtlety isn't exactly their strong suit," Ben said with a mirthless chuckle. "Speaking of subtlety… Christmas card? Really? I can't believe Marlee fell for such a lame ploy."

She snickered, flexing her fingers on the steering wheel. "Marlee didn't fall for anything. I promise you she knew I was trying to get in touch with Harry."

"Why? Does it have something to do with the Coulter case?"

Alicia took a deep breath in, then let it out slowly. She wasn't a fan of other people digging into her business, but if there was anyone in Pine Bluff she trusted, it was Ben Kinsella. They'd trained together when they first started with the DEA. And later, she'd been equally impressed and outraged on his behalf when the agency hung him out to dry. Ben had been forced to give up both his career and his life in Atlanta when he got crossways with one of the most influential gang leaders in the state, but he'd landed on his feet. Now she was staring down the possibility of needing to start from scratch, and not sure she'd handle it as gracefully.

"No. Um… Let's say there's some unresolved personal business between Harrison Hayes and me and leave it at that," she said cagily.

Ben let out a bull-like snort. "I may not have twigged to the Christmas-card thing, but I figured the rest out on my own."

"Yeah, well, I don't think it's the right time or place for me to give you the details, so let's file this under It's Complicated."

"Okay," Ben said cautiously. "But you're all right, correct?"

"Other than exposure to a fake toxin and someone mistaking me for a buck in season?" she asked tartly.

"Yeah, other than those things."

"I am." She let her head fall back against the headrest as she scanned the miles of empty state highway ahead of her. "I'm actually more than okay. I think."

"As clear as mud," Ben grumbled. "But I guess you'll tell me what's going on in your own time."

"I will." She drummed her fingers on the steering wheel and then sat up straighter in her seat. "I'm heading into the office in Atlanta this afternoon, but I expect I may be spending some more time in Pine Bluff as we get closer to the trial."

"Oh? I would have figured you'd moved on to another case by now," Ben said, a note of concern creeping into his voice.

"Yeah, well, Bronson has me working on a number of cases," she said, hoping the frustration she'd been feeling for the past couple of months didn't ring through in her tone.

"How are things with the new section chief?"

Alicia avoided pressing any harder on the accelerator as she felt the tension creep from her shoulders up to her neck. Funny, in the past twelve hours she'd been shot at, tackled a guy, been flipped and pinned down and thoroughly dusted in what they all hoped was nothing more than cornstarch, but she hadn't felt this kind of searing tension the mere thought of her new boss conjured. It still galled her Andrew Bronson had snagged the section-chief job. It should have been hers, and they both knew it. Ticked her off even more he had the power to assign her to tasks that were essentially a waste of her time and talents. Heaven forbid she might show him up.

"About as you'd expect," she said briefly.

Ben knew better than anyone how bad things might end up being for her. The agency had used him up and tossed him aside once his cover was blown. Alicia had no illusions about her own position. There were people gunning for her. Had been since she'd been promoted ahead of most of the guys she came up with. Andrew Bronson was more than old-school. He was almost a throwback to another era. The era where men did not welcome women into their ranks.

And he had her sighted in his crosshairs.

"Don't worry about me," she said to Ben. "He's not the first jerk boss I've ever had. He won't be the last."

"If he doesn't value his best agent, then he's an idiot," Ben grumbled.

Alicia smiled. Her personnel file had to gall Bronson. She had more commendations and better performance reviews than any of the male agents in his section. Every day, he found some sneaky way to make it clear he didn't like women on the job. More than once he'd alluded to the supposed emotional instability of females. Of course, he'd always been talking about the women caught up on the other side of their cases. In an odd way, Alicia couldn't help thinking Bronson liked women best when they were pawns or unwitting witnesses. He saw most women as nothing more than tools used to bring big men down. It certainly irked him to believe a mere woman might be able to see through him, much less outmaneuver him.

Six months ago, she wouldn't have worried over her job for one minute, but now... Now her present situation felt more precarious. Once he found out she was pregnant, it would be open season on her career. As much as she hated what was happening to Harrison Hayes and his Podunk town, Alicia couldn't help but see the threats being made against him as an opportunity for her to step out of Bronson's line of sight long enough to figure out her next move.

"I'm going to gather more in-depth information on what you've given me and put it together with what we have on file for Coulter. The last thing Bronson wants is for such a high-profile collar to slither out from under these charges, so I'm going to see if I can make a case for staying in Pine Bluff for a few weeks."

"I see." Ben spoke the words quietly and with almost no inflection, but she knew he understood what she was saying.

Alicia had been one of the few agents to reach out to Ben after the agency turned its back on him. She needn't spell out her situation for him. If she was willing to duck out of the Atlanta office and all of the plum assignments she could be snagging, Ben would twig to the notion everything wasn't as peachy as she'd like it to be.

She gripped the wheel tighter and shrugged, even though Ben couldn't see her attempt at bravado. "Maybe Bronson will be happy to have me out of sight and mind for a while."

"I can ask Marlee to see if the house we set you up in last time is still available," he offered.

Alicia's memory flashed on the pretty brass bed tucked under the eaves of the bungalow she'd invited Harrison Hayes to one cool autumn night, and a prickle of perspiration tickled her hairline. She swiped the back of her hand across her forehead.

"Thank you, but I think I'm gonna stick closer to Hayes if I can," she replied, trying to keep her tone light and casual, but all too aware he could see through her casual tone.

"Exactly how close are you planning to stick?" Ben pressed.

"His guest room is pretty comfortable. Nice plush

pillow-top mattress," she said with a small smile.
"The rest of the decor is a bit austere. More a monk's
cell than a guest room, but I guess one can't expect
much more from a confirmed bachelor."

"You plan on staying at Hayes's house?"

The disbelief in his voice gave her a moment to
pause, but she'd lain awake half the night thinking
this plan through. She could move in. She would be
able to keep a closer eye on Harry, plus it would give
them the opportunity to talk through what needed to
come next for them. She could help keep him safe
and acquire a legitimized hole for her to hide out in
until she figured out exactly how to approach her
career conundrum.

"Is Harry in on this, or did you make a unilat-
eral decision to move into his place?" Ben's question
jolted her from her thoughts.

"He isn't on board yet, but I don't think he's going
to object too strenuously," she said with a confidence
she didn't quite feel. "Anyway, I can't do anything
until I get back to the office to assess our situation,
add these notes to the file and run it past Bronson."

"You'll keep me updated?" the sheriff asked.

"Ten-four," she replied succinctly.

"Be safe, Alicia. Don't worry about things here.
We're keeping a close eye on Harry. I truly believe
most of what's happening is meant to scare him more
than harm him."

"It scared me, and this is not the first time I've
been under direct fire," she reminded him. "You

guys may believe this is nothing but a bunch of the hayseeds blowing off steam, but I'm looking at it as something more serious. Hopefully, between the two of us, we'll get it right."

"Call me after you talk to Bronson. If we need to, I can have Marlee apply some pressure to have agency representation here. We can also get Representative Wingate to weigh in if we need to."

Ben's girlfriend, Marlee Masters, ran Timber Masters, the county's largest employer. She was a powerful woman with a lot of pull. Pull Ben had no trouble taking advantage of when it served the greater good.

"Keep your big guns holstered for now, Sheriff. I'll send up a flare if I can't handle the chief myself," she promised. Alicia ended the call and blew out a long breath. If she wasn't misreading him, she'd bet anything Bronson would be as happy to get rid of her for a while as she would be to get lost.

She was wrong in her assessment. For a split second, Andrew Bronson looked to be ecstatic at the prospect of having her out from under his feet for a while. Then he remembered if he said yes, he'd be giving her what she wanted, and shut her down.

"You are working on a number of crucial cases for us," he said officiously.

Alicia wanted to sneer. He had her sifting through raw video footage and unedited audio collected from undercover operatives in hopes of unearthing nuggets of gold. A task which would keep her tied to her desk and mired in the minutiae of a handful of cases, rather than letting her sink her teeth into one.

Her former chief was Bronson's polar opposite. Waterson appreciated her doggedness, but also allowed her to run with her gut instincts. When she'd made the connection between some of the jail-house ramblings of deceased Atlanta drug kingpin Ivan Jones and indications that heroin was moving through the rural parts of the state using the loose network of locals, she'd started poking around to see if she could locate the source of distribution. And there he was: Samuel "Cottonmouth" Coulter. Eccentric millionaire, friend to some of South Florida's most elusive importers, exotic snake collector and general bad guy.

She'd led the charge down into Masters County. She'd collected the evidence against him, following every single breadcrumb Coulter had dropped since he moved from Miami to Jacksonville and then finally into Georgia. She was the one who made this happen. She didn't need some jackass coming in at the eleventh hour telling her she couldn't do her part to keep the prosecutorial team safe.

"Understood," she said, keeping her response to a minimum so she wouldn't risk mouthing off. "But, Chief, I'm still connected in the area. I have contacts who will set me up. I can keep a low profile, mostly undercover. I want to do whatever I can to help the local authorities apprehend these troublemakers before things can get too serious."

"Don't they have law enforcement there?" He raised his eyebrows in challenge. "I thought I heard your old friend Ben Kinsella had landed down there? He's county sheriff now, isn't he?"

Alicia heard the derision in the man's tone but refused to be baited. "Yes, Ben is about to be elected to a full term and seems happy in Pine Bluff," she replied, as if responding to a polite inquiry.

"Well, then, I'm sure someone as…capable as your friend Ben can keep a lid on things."

Unwilling to be dismissed so easily, she pressed on. "I looked into a few of the groups operating in the area and some have crossed paths with us on previous occasions. If the brass need justification beyond keeping the people working Coulter's case safe, we can tell them I'm looking into deeper connections between some of the militia groups in the distribution network."

"We are already looking at them." It was a lie, but she couldn't call him on it. He was her superior, and if he said it was under control, she was supposed to accept his word at face value. Bronson tapped the top of his desk, then nodded to the door. "Don't you worry about it. All you need to do is be prepared to testify when the time comes. Otherwise, I need you here. You're the best I have when it comes to finding those tiny needles in the haystacks."

Alicia shot up out of her chair and made a beeline for the ladies' room. It had been all she could do to keep her breakfast down through her chat with her boss.

She didn't dare take more than five minutes to rinse her mouth, wash her hands and shake a few mints out of the container she'd started carrying in her pocket. It was ridiculous, but being the only female in her section made her self-conscious about anything the men she worked with might consider feminine. She needed to figure out a way to get back to Masters County. Preferably in some sort of official capacity so she didn't have to worry about burning up leave she could be banking for the weeks after the baby was born. But she wasn't going to get anything done by hiding out in the ladies' room.

Winding her way through the warren of low-walled cubicles, she turned a corner to find Alan Campbell hovering nearby. She eyed the other agent warily as she approached. Campbell had transferred from another division and wasn't as entrenched in the desire to outpace her as some of the men she'd come up with seemed to be. Still, they weren't exactly friends. It had taken only a few weeks under Bronson's command to make it clear she was the agent on the outside looking in at the good old boys' club. She wasn't entirely certain where Campbell fell on the scale of tolerable to insufferable.

Slowing her steps, she forced a small smile because heaven forbid she come off as unfriendly or uncooperative. "Hey, Campbell," she greeted him. "Something you needed?"

The other agent nodded. "The chief said I might want to send you some files to listen to."

Alicia clenched her teeth in her effort to keep her smile in place. This was the kind of garbage detail she'd been getting lately. Of course, whenever anyone pressed Bronson about why his most decorated agent was spending her time culling through hours of grainy footage or muffled voice recordings, he simply beamed and told anyone listening she was the *absolute best* when it came down to *fine detail* work, and he was only making sure he put his *ace* on the job.

For his part, Campbell seemed completely oblivious to her agitation. "There's something there. I can feel it. There's something I'm hearing, but not quite getting."

He ran a frustrated hand through already rumpled hair, and she lowered the flame under her indignation. The appeal in his eyes made it clear he actually had come to her in hopes she might be able to ping on exactly what it was he was missing. Inhaling deeply through her nose, she moved past him to her desk and dropped into her chair.

"Oh yeah? What have you got?"

"We've got a guy who's been in with some of the local low-level operatives." The section chief's preferred term for gang members who worked the trade on the streets. "A couple of them were members in the southeast crew we thought were scattered to the winds a couple years ago."

Alicia sat up straighter, fighting to keep her mask of casual indifference firmly in place. She was excited by a connection he might have to the mostly disbanded gang, but refused to let it show. For years, the Southeast Atlanta gang had been ruled by a man named Ivan Jones. Ivan liked to think he was the drug kingpin of the southeastern United States, though there were many in the underworld who would argue the title shouldn't apply to anyone who moved low-grade inventory like methamphetamine.

Still, Ivan and his network had been a big deal to the DEA. So big, Ben Kinsella, former DEA agent and current Masters County sheriff, had once been deeply embedded in the man's organization. But Ben's mission to take Jones down barely qualified as a success. Sure, they'd locked the guy up in the end, but a number of people were killed, and Ben's cover had been blown wide open. Poor Ben had watched his best friend die during the raid to take Jones down. He'd also ended up with a bounty on his head, making him expendable to the agency.

"What makes you think they could be connected to the Southeast gang?" she asked Campbell.

"They said so," he said with a shrug.

"Then what do you need me for?"

"I think whatever they have going is connected to something bigger."

Intrigued, she gestured to the single guest chair she kept nearby. "Connected in what way?"

"They said something about Ivan's lawyer and some land downstate." He shrugged again. "They were talking about how the guy had died and left everything all, uh, screwed up, but then someone stepped in."

"Someone stepped in where?" she asked.

He shook his head. "I'm not exactly sure. And I may only be drawing all these lines in my head, but I was wondering... What was the name of the town where you arrested Samuel Coulter?"

Chapter Six

Dusty's Barbecue was a Masters County mainstay. Nestled in a notch cut out of timber-company woods, the shack near the highway overpass had served some of the best smoked meats in South Georgia for over thirty years. It was also the only place in the county with a liquor license allowing for on-premises consumption. After having his place busted up a couple of times in the early days, Dusty decided to limit his alcoholic offerings to long-necked bottles of beer and a couple of cheap wines no one ever ordered, but his wife seemed to like.

Since dining options in the area were severely limited and the barbecue joint was the only public place a body could walk in and order a cold beer, most everyone visited Dusty's at some time or another. Harry made his way there on the night after Alicia Simmons dropped her bomb on his life.

Behind the bar, Dusty's daughter Selena pulled a bottle from the ice bath and uncapped it with a quick flick of her wrist. When he was a boy, Harry had thought she was incredibly strong. Now he knew she kept a small metal bottle opener practically embedded in her palm as she worked her shift.

"Thanks, Sel," he said as she slid the bottle in front of him.

"You eating?" she asked, propping her knuckles on her hip and eyeing him speculatively. "Ribs are long gone, but we have the pork sandwich plate on special today."

Twirling the bottle until the label faced him, Harry considered the meager options in his fridge, then gave her a nod. "Sounds good. Beans and slaw for my sides, please and thank you."

"Coming right up."

Bottle in hand, Harry spun on his stool and took a moment to peer into the wood-on-wood gloom of the place. Signs advertising beverages or food specials provided the only color. Aside from the patrons. Dusty's was a veritable treasure trove for a person who enjoyed people watching. And Harry did. Now, with the workday wrapping up, the restaurant and bar was as full as it would ever be past the lunchtime rush.

Most of the men who worked the mills in the area stopped at Dusty's for a cold one on their way home. Harry recognized a good many of them. There were a couple of strangers in leather biker gear lounging at a table in the corner. They had the wind-beaten cragginess of men who spent a great deal of time on the road. He spotted Darleen Sheridan from the Daisy Drive-In sitting with Patti Cummings. Patti's overprocessed blond hair shone like a beacon as the two women huddled close, their expressions avid. There must be hot news in town, Harry concluded. He made a mental note to prime the gossip pump with a trip to the Daisy the next day. People tended to dismiss gossip as petty and avoid the town busybodies, but he didn't. The lumber mills provided the residents with a livelihood, but Pine Bluff's thriving gossip mill kept track of everything and everyone else in their lives.

Harry knew Arnie and Andy Smithson were regulars at Dusty's. Sure enough, when he scanned the patrons scattered around the scarred wooden tables, he spotted the brothers. It would have been hard to miss them. They were seated with a whole crowd of people wearing Timber Masters logos on their uniform shirts and jackets. They'd pushed three tables together to make one long one stretching across the rear wall of the building. The Smithsons sat with their backs to the wall and their gazes locked on him.

He braced his elbows on the bar and let the beer bottle dangle from his fingers. The scrape of chair legs on the wooden plank floor didn't bother him. Nor was he afraid of the large man stretching himself to his full height. As he'd explained to Alicia, he had known Arnie and his younger brother Andy his whole life. Regardless of Arnie's somewhat checkered past and reputation as a hothead, Harry found it hard to be afraid of someone he knew so well.

He quirked a smile as the mountain of a man approached. Arnie's curling gray-brown beard had grown out a bit. Harry couldn't help wondering if the foreman was stretching the limitations on Timber Masters safety policies concerning facial hair. Maybe he'd mention something to Marlee in passing. A joke about old Arnie gunning for Santa Claus's job or something. 'Twas the season, after all.

Harry lifted his bottle of beer a couple of inches in salute when the other man drew to a stop a few feet away. "Evening, Arnie."

"Heard you got your house shot up," Smithson replied, crossing his bulky arms over his barrel chest.

Harry gave his head a rueful shake. "You know, I got the porch repainted in September. Makes me mad when people make me do work twice."

"Yeah, well, I don't know what theories you and your friend the sheriff have cooked up, but it wasn't me or mine," Arnie replied resolutely. "So if you're here thinking you can shake us down for some kind of confession, you're barking up the wrong tree."

"Shake you down," Harry said with a laugh. Raising the bottle of beer to his lips, he kept his eyes fixed on the bigger man as he took a pull of the icy cold brew. "Seems foolish for a man like me to try to shake a man like you, and we both know I'm not foolish." Harrison maintained eye contact. "You may not have pulled the trigger, but I'm willing to bet you know who did."

"I'm not allowed to gamble these days," Arnie replied. "You know Annelle would have my head."

Harry smirked. Once upon a time, Arnie had been busted for trying to knock over a Prescott County gas station with a pointing finger in his jacket pocket. Apparently, he put some money on a football game, and Arnie couldn't pay up when his team hadn't pulled through. Unfortunately, he was wearing his work coat with his name embroidered on the front. A lenient judge gave him six months for the attempt. But for nearly a decade, the man had to endure the jokes about finger-pistol desperadoes.

"Annelle is a smart woman. I always wondered what she saw in you," Harry said, tossing off the insult with a friendly smile.

"You can keep on wondering," Arnie said, his smile not quite as friendly but still there. "Let's say she doesn't love me for my brains."

"That much has been obvious for years." He took another sip of his beer.

"I wanted to come over and tell you man-to-man it wasn't us," Arnie said, jerking his head toward a small knot of men seated at his table. "You know if we had a beef with you, we'd come right at you."

He quirked an eyebrow. "Did I hear you threaten an officer of the court?"

Arnie was smart enough to shake his head. "Nope. I was very careful to pose a hypothetical."

Pleased with himself, the big man pivoted and walked back to his table of friends. Harry studied each of them for a moment. A couple of faces were familiar, though he couldn't quite put names with them.

If they became a bigger concern, he could put some feelers out with Marlee Masters and see if her supervisors hadn't heard any rumblings about them.

His gaze connected with Andy Smithson, and the two men who had known each other their entire lives, gone through twelve years of school together and even gotten drunk in this very bar together, shared a moment of unspoken communication. When Andy raised his eyebrows, Harry could do nothing but nod in acquiescence. He believed them. Which made it worse, because now he had absolutely no idea who might be taking potshots at his house.

Sighing, Harry took a long pull on his bottle of beer. A plate clattered onto the bar behind him. He spun on the stool to find a sectioned plate piled high with piping-hot barbecue waiting for him, and his stomach growled its approval.

He flashed another smile at Selena and swung around on his stool. "Looks good."

She deposited a tightly wrapped bundle of silverware and a couple of packets containing moist towelettes beside the plate, then wiped her hands on a dishcloth. "Best damn barbecue around," she replied flippantly before returning to the kitchen.

Harry focused his attention on the heaping plate of food in front of him. The scent of hickory smoke and tangy sauce made his mouth water. Picking up the roll of silverware, he unfurled a napkin he knew would be unequal to the task at hand and placed it on his lap, then grabbed his fork.

Sauce-drenched pulled pork stood high and proud atop the bottom half of an oversize bun. He shoveled up a heaping helping of slaw, dumped it on top of the meat and smooshed the top half of the bun down until the good stuff oozed out the sides.

Pleased to get his hands dirty with something other than criminal matters, he picked up the sandwich and took a healthy bite. Harry could feel the sauce smears clinging to his lips and cheeks, but didn't bother swiping them away. There'd only be more where those came from, and he liked to wait until the job was done to clean up right.

As he worked his way through the sandwich, he tried to let his mind drift, but it kept jolting over the speed bumps set out by the previous evening's events.

He'd been happy to see Alicia Simmons at his door. As happy as he'd been sad when she left Pine Bluff without saying goodbye. Not heartbroken, but maybe mildly disappointed? They were both grown-ups and knew going in what they would be to one another. Or thought they knew.

Pregnant.

The word kept popping into his head like one of those plastic moles you tried to beat down with a foam mallet at an arcade.

His chewing slowed and Harry set the sandwich carefully back on the plate. He had to swallow hard to get the food down. Alicia Simmons was pregnant with his child. Oddly enough, he'd never really doubted her word the baby was his. He had a hard enough time wrapping his head around the existence of a baby at all. But Alicia was nothing if not a straight shooter. He'd believed her the minute it all came tumbling out. He simply didn't know how to process the information.

He was gonna be a father. Thoughts had ricocheted around in his mind all day, but he hadn't been able to grasp one of them long enough to figure out how he felt about it. He planned on being a father one day. It might not have been happening in the way he expected, but this wasn't a bad thing. Most things didn't come about the way a person expected. He sure wouldn't have counted on being the last member of his family left in Pine Bluff, for one thing.

But here he was, back in the place he once yearned to escape. Back by choice, not circumstance, like Marlee Masters. He'd moved back with this brand-spanking-new law degree and happily taken the job as the assistant district attorney for the area.

His parents had been shocked. His sister incredulous. He had no way of explaining to them what had caused the change of heart because he wasn't quite sure himself. All he knew was when he saw the job posting pop up, he jumped at it without hesitation.

Harry rocked back on the stool and sucked the barbecue sauce off each of his fingers before reaching for the napkin on his lap to dry them. He sighed and ducked his head, bracing his forearms on the edge of the bar. The fact was, the minute Alicia had said she was going back to Atlanta, he'd wanted to protest, though he knew he didn't have a right. He wanted her here, even if it was irrational to think she'd stay. Alicia had a career there. A damn good one. She had decorations and commendations. He assumed she had a life there, as well. He wasn't exactly the social butterfly of Masters County, but he had friends. She likely did too. And those friends certainly weren't going to be pointing her in the direction of a small-time prosecutor who chose to live in the middle of nowhere.

After picking up his fork, Harry scooped up some baked beans and shoveled in a few mouthfuls. He ate on autopilot, oblivious to the noise and commotion around him. Within a few minutes, he'd demolished the beans and what was left of the slaw and the sandwich, not giving them the appreciation they deserved.

"Must've been good," someone commented gruffly.

Harry jerked and his head swiveled. Ben Kinsella stood behind him. Still chewing, Harry eyeballed the sheriff. "Evening," he said, but with more warmth than he'd given Arnie Smithson. He took in the jeans, flannel and ball cap the other man wore and nodded to the empty stool beside him. "I take it you're off duty tonight?"

Ben gave a brief nod as he straddled the stool. "Picking up some barbecue. I find it helps to have food on hand if I hope to lure Marlee away from the office anytime before seven."

"Smart thinking." Harry tore open a wet wipe and used it to give his face and hands a thorough cleaning. "Had a chat with Arnie," he said, gesturing toward the long table before the sheriff could ask. "I don't think it was them."

Ben bobbed his head, then smiled at Selena as she approached. "Hey, Selena. I need two of the specials with potato salad and beans to go."

She nodded and made a note on her pad. "Want a drink while you wait?" she asked, pointing her pen to Harry's beer bottle.

"Don't mind if I do."

She uncapped a cold one and slid it in front of the sheriff. "Another, Harry?"

He shook his head. "I'm good. I'm driving, and I hear the law around here is pretty vigilant."

Ben smirked as he lifted his bottle and toasted them both with it. "It's a tough town. Somebody got his house shot up last night."

Selena, who'd started for the kitchen, stopped short, spun on her heel, then marched back over to them. The stern expression on her face had Harry and Ben pulling up straight as she leaned in to speak to them under the din. "What did you say?"

Ben lowered his bottle to the bar, then spoke with deliberation. "Someone took a few potshots at Harry's house last night. Took out the porch light. Almost took out a friend of ours."

A deep furrow appeared between Selena's brows. She glanced over at Harry, her expression surprising him. She looked torn between incredulity and anger. "Are you kidding me? Actually shot at your house?"

Ben spoke before Harry could. "Yes."

She planted her hands on her hips and rocked back on her heels, clearly weighing something in her mind. At last, she pitched forward again. "I wasn't going to say anything because, you know, I hear things—all sorts of things—but I never know what's true or not."

"We understand," Ben prompted, glancing over at Harry as if looking for confirmation of his presumption.

Harry nodded. "Anything you've heard might help." He balled up the wrapper from the wet wipe and tossed it onto his empty plate. "I'd appreciate it. I really liked my porch light."

She scowled so fiercely Harry was afraid he'd pushed too hard, but then she shook her head, clearly disgusted. "Not those two in the corner," she said, flicking a glance toward the bikers seated at the corner table. "But I'm seeing more and more guys from that, uh, club come through these days."

Neither Harry nor Ben was dumb enough to look, but Harry recalled the men he'd spotted when scanning the room. "The bikers?"

"The Outriders," she said with a sneer in her voice. "Not even a good name."

Her commentary coaxed a reluctant laugh from Harry. "Aw, come on. It's not bad."

"Only saying they could have done better," Selena said, raising her hands as if to ward off an argument.

Ben wasn't as easily distracted. "The Outriders," he murmured as he automatically reached for the notebook he kept in the breast pocket of his uniform shirt. Unfortunately, the patch pockets on his flannel were empty. "Damn."

Harry pulled his phone out of his pocket and sent a text message with the name. "There. And I want it noted technology saved the day for you in this case. You're the only person I know who is even more low-tech than I am."

Ben rolled his eyes, then checked his own phone to be sure he had the information. Lifting his bottle, he flashed Selena a smile so mild they might have been exchanging recipes. "How many would you guess you've seen lately?"

Selena pursed her lips and shrugged. "At least a half dozen, but likely more. Usually come in twos or threes. No big groups, like a club out for a cruise, you know?"

"Gotcha. Thanks, Sel. We'll put some feelers out." He took a sip of his beer as she headed back to the kitchen again.

But Harry saw a spark of something restless in Selena's eyes. On impulse, he called after her. "Hey, Selena?" When she spun around, quirking one perfectly arched brow, he gave her the winsome smile he used to woo a jury. "I, uh—" he made a motion to imply she should keep their conversation on the down low "—appreciate your help."

Running her tongue over her teeth, she marched back over to them, tore a ticket from her pad and said, "Put your money where your mouth is, Mr. District Attorney."

Laughing, Harry reached for his wallet as the swinging door swooped back and forth in her wake. "She's gonna start nosing around," he said without looking at Ben.

Ben nodded, then tossed off Harry's worry with a shrug. "You know as well as I do service personnel are some of the best sources any investigation can have."

"I don't want her asking too many questions and getting unwelcome attention. Selena has her hands full running this place and trying to keep old Dusty from working himself to death. She doesn't need to be doing our jobs, as well."

"Well, for your information, I *have* been doing my job, Counselor." Ben grasped the neck of his bottle and tipped it toward him, rolling the edge of the bottom back and forth. "I've identified a handful of credible leads as to who might have you in their sights."

"Oh yeah?" Harry threw a twenty down on top of the ticket to cover his meal, the single beer and allow for about a 60 percent tip.

A minute later, Selena came through the swinging door again holding a tightly wrapped plastic bag with two food containers. She swept Harry's ticket and the twenty from the counter. "Need change?"

"Doubt I'd get it even if I said yes," he answered with a smirk.

She flashed a smile. "Have a good night," she said dismissively, then slapped a ticket down in front of Ben.

Harry clapped a hand on Ben's shoulder as he rose. "Wow. No freebies for the law around here."

"No freebies in Dusty's at all," Selena retorted. "Never have been, never will be."

The sheriff shook his head as he pulled out his wallet and extracted a card. "And worth every penny," he said with an affable smile. "Night, Harry."

Harry let his gaze drift to the table along the back wall before sweeping the room. The two biker guys in the corner were still there, their table littered with wadded napkins and several empty beer bottles, and their gazes fixed on the sheriff. Harry figured they'd let Ben get a head start before mounting their rides. Probably hoping to evade any chance at being pulled over.

Pushing through the door, he hunkered into his suit coat, though the worsted wool did little to inhibit the chilly wind. He was halfway to his car before he spotted the trouble. There she sat, his poor, abused car. Her shiny—if slightly marred on one side—paint job gleaming in the floodlights illuminating the parking area. All four of his tires were flat.

There was a short burst of noise and clatter as someone came out the door, but soon the evening quiet closed in around him again. Before he managed to pick which swear word to use, a heavy hand landed on his shoulder.

Anger and frustration roiled inside him as he saw Ben staring mournfully at his BMW. "Come on," the other man said gruffly. "I'll give you a lift home."

Chapter Seven

It took everything she could glean from Campbell's recordings plus the information she'd received from Ben Kinsella, but Alicia was finally able to convince Bronson to let her head back to Pine Bluff. A well-placed word in his superior's ear hadn't hurt either. At last, he set her free to see for herself what was happening with her case down in Masters County.

She pulled to a stop in front of Harry's house exactly where she'd parked mere days before. The neighborhood looked much the same. A few people had started decorating for Christmas, giving the street a boost of much-needed color as the days grew shorter and the nights longer. She noted Harry had compensated for his broken porch light by stringing white Christmas lights along porch rails and pillars. They should have cheered her, but the thought of him standing out there hanging those lights, open to any crackpot with a gun, made her stomach flip over.

Slamming the car door, she strode around to the trunk and hefted the suitcase she'd barely touched since her last trip to Pine Bluff. Once upon a time, she rarely fully unpacked from any trip. Before Bronson had become her chief, she was hardly in the office for more than two days together. She'd come home, send out a batch of dry cleaning or run a couple of loads of laundry, then put everything back into the same suitcase and go.

But whether Bronson clipped her wings or not, those days were over for her. Or at least they would be soon. Soon, she would be planted. She'd finally let her roots sink into the soil so her child would know who he or she was and where he or she came from and never face the sort of displacement she had as an army brat.

After setting the suitcase on the asphalt, she extended the handle and dragged it up over the curb with a grunt. She noted the lack of car in the drive, but figured the lights on inside were a good indicator. Maybe Harry had finally decided to use his garage as an actual garage. The luggage wheels bumped over the grassy berm until she reached the walkway leading to his front door. At the foot of the steps, she abandoned the extension and reached for the handle attached to the top of the case to heft it up the four shallow stairs.

The weight of the case hitting the wooden floorboards must have alerted Harry to a caller, because the foyer light went on. She pressed the bell, but the door swung open before she could retract her finger.

"Alicia," he said gruffly. "What are you doing here?"

She took a moment to appreciate the view. He wasn't wearing a suit coat, but he wore gray pin-striped trousers and a white shirt with his polished wing tips. His collar was open, and any evidence of a tie had been eradicated. Dark stubble shadowed the distinct lines of his jaw.

Alicia smiled, recalling how upon meeting him for the first time she'd decided his slightly pointy nose kept him from being too blandly handsome. Harrison Hayes was one of those men who snuck up on you. His charm and appeal lay as much in his sharp mind, quick wit and sly smile as it did his good looks. One might be tempted to dismiss him as simply yet another clean-cut Southern man with his neatly trimmed hair and solemn hazel eyes. But dismissing Harry for any reason was a mistake. It took Alicia about twenty-four hours to realize the district attorney grew far more potent as one got to know him.

"I'm coming to stay for a while," she announced.

He rolled a pointed glance down at the suitcase beside her and raised an eyebrow. "So I see."

"I mean, I'm coming to stay with you," she said, clarifying.

His head jerked up and he looked genuinely surprised by the notion. "Coming to stay with me?"

She gave a brisk nod. "May I come in? It's cold out here."

Ever the gentleman, Harry unlatched the screen door and pushed it open. Then he stepped back, allowing her to pass. When she reached for her suit-case, his hand closed over hers. "I'll get your bag."

She didn't fight him, because mainly she was tired of wrestling with the damn thing. If he wanted to be all chivalrous about things, she wasn't about to stop him. Once they were inside with the door closed firmly behind them, Harry glanced down at the large suitcase again before looking her dead in the eye.

"You think you're going to stay with me?"

"Ben offered the house I had before, but I don't see much point since I plan to stick pretty close to you the next couple weeks."

His jaw dropped and his eyes opened so wide she almost laughed. He was the very caricature of a man in shock. "You do?"

"I've been assigned to investigate some of the threats being made against you in the weeks lead-ing up to the Coulter trial."

"Everybody and their brother is already investi-gating most threats. Why did they need to send you?"

"You act like you aren't happy to see me." She planted a hand on her hip and thrust it to the side as she studied him directly. "Would you prefer I leave?"

He shook his head. "No."

His answer came quick enough to assure her it was his gut reaction, so she rolled with it. "We've come across some indicators leading us in a differ-ent direction when it comes to identifying the forces behind the perpetrators of these crimes."

"Crimes?" He gave a brief, bitter laugh. "Around

here, we call it mischief and vow to get even with whoever it was later."

"Where I'm from, it's called terroristic threatening." She smiled then. "Potato, po-tah-to."

Harry ran his hand through his hair, rumpling its styled perfection. The nervous habit had been one of the things that first drew her to him. Alicia found tousled Harry so appealing she'd once reached over and smoothed his hair in the middle of their post-interrogation recap. She wanted to mess him up now, but doing so wouldn't be appropriate. Which was ironic, considering they knew each other a lot more intimately now than they had then.

"Come in," he said, gesturing toward the living room. "I'll, uh, put this in the guest room."

She smiled to herself as he wheeled her bag away. In the living room, she took a minute to drink in the details of the room she hadn't bothered noticing the night they were under fire.

Framed family photos were arrayed atop side tables and on a couple of floating shelves attached to the wall. The room was furnished with comfortable, masculine pieces upholstered in leather. An old refinished trunk served as the coffee table, and an upright piano was installed against the far wall.

"Would you like something to drink?" Harry called from the hallway.

"Water is fine, thank you."

A moment later he reappeared with two bottles of water in hand. He loosened the cap on one before handing it to her. Alicia smiled, once again amused. "Thank you. I never would've been able to open a bottle on my own."

"Oh, sorry. Habit," he said with a shrug.

"You often go around handing out bottled water?" She eyed him as she lifted the bottle to her lips and took a quick sip, trying to figure out this somewhat inscrutable man.

He shook his head. "No, but my mama taught me to serve people a certain way. I wouldn't dare hand a can of Coca-Cola without first popping the top."

Alicia laughed. "I see. Yes, heaven forbid we risk a broken fingernail."

He smiled as he joined her on the sofa, leaving the cushion between them open, but angling his body to face hers. "I know you're tough, but like I said, old habits."

"I understand." She gestured to the array of photos. "Does your family live nearby?"

He shook his head. "My sister and her family live in the Chicago area. My parents retired to Florida."

"It always kind of tickles me when people move from Georgia down to Florida. Doesn't seem to me like there'd be a whole lot of difference."

"Maybe not from Atlanta to Florida, but there's a whole world of difference between Masters County and most cities in Florida."

"Your father was a doctor, right?"

He raised his bottle to her in silent salute. "You've been doing your research." He took a drink, then nodded. "My father was general practitioner here in town, and my mother was a homemaker, though she wasn't much interested in housework. She spent most of her days down at the beauty parlor catching up on the latest. My sister is also a doctor, as is her husband. I am the black sheep."

A laugh burbled out of her. "If the black sheep ends up being a successful district attorney, I'd say your family is doing quite well."

He shrugged. "Anyway, they all seem happy, and I'm happy here, so I guess we're all winning at life." He propped his elbow on the back of the sofa and rested the bottle on his thigh. "How about you? Where's your family?"

Alicia's smile faded. "Let's see." She tipped her head back. "At the moment, my parents are in Germany, but they're due back into the Washington, DC, area sometime after the first of the year." She straightened and eyed him directly. "My father is expected to take an appointment with the Joint Chiefs of Staff."

He did a comical double take. "Joint Chiefs of Staff? Wow. Cool."

"The culmination of a lifetime of work."

"Which branch?"

"Army."

"Any siblings?"

She shook her head. "No, only me. They found out pretty quickly a child can slow a person down when one is trying to march up the ladder."

"I see." His face softened.

Alicia shrugged his sympathy off. There was no sense fretting over it. Her childhood was long over. She had her own life and her own career to worry about. Her relationship with her parents was fine, if somewhat distant. Frankly, it suited her as well as it suited them. And there was no sense dwelling on the past when she had a future to plan.

"So, I did go to the doctor, and the pregnancy is confirmed." He sat back, and his face went blank. She didn't know if his sudden reserve was due to the subject matter or the abrupt shift in conversation topics, but if they were going to work out any sort of relationship, she believed they needed to have all their cards out on the table. "I didn't count right, though. I'm actually almost eight weeks along, but everything seems to be right on target."

Her brisk summation earned her a slight change in expression, but for the most part, he was still unreadable. This was the problem with dealing with lawyers—their poker faces were too damn good.

"I thought you should know," she said, opening her hands in a gesture she hoped he'd read as simple frankness.

As if snapped from a trance, Harry ran his hand over his face, a gesture she was coming to recognize as his way of grounding himself before speaking. "Okay. Well, wow." He chuckled. "I guess it shouldn't come as such a shock to hear again, but it does." He cocked his head and gave her a crooked smile. "You're pregnant."

She nodded solemnly, a responsive smile quirked at her lips. "I am indeed."

"Have you thought any about how you're going to handle it work-wise?" he asked.

"I have," she replied thoughtfully. "I'm not going to lie. It's going to be complicated."

"To say the least," he said with a laugh. As if the situation were only dawning on him, his whole face brightened. "Wow. I can't believe this is happening."

She narrowed her eyes. "Going by your facial expression, I'm guessing this isn't an entirely unwelcome turn of events in your life?"

He shook his head. "No. It isn't. Unexpected, yes. But I've had time to digest...and not unwelcome."

She took a moment to absorb his assurance. "Does this mean you *do* want to be involved in some way?"

He answered without hesitation. "Yes."

She almost jumped out of her skin when he reached across and took her free hand in his.

"Alicia, I know the situation isn't ideal, and was unplanned, but I thought about it a lot over the past couple of days, and one thing I am *not* is unhappy. As a matter of fact, given everything going on around here, this may be the best news I've had in weeks."

His sincerity unleashed a flood of warmth she hadn't realized she was repressing. Flipping her hand over, she gave his fingers a gentle squeeze. "I'm glad you're happy. Like I told you before, this might've been an accident, but it's a happy accident, in my book. I'm glad it's one for you too."

He let out a nervous laugh as she released his hand and drew back. She watched as he laced his long, graceful fingers together and let them dangle between them. "Okay, so you're here. You're here working. You're pregnant, and you intend to live in my house while you're here working." He shot her a sidelong glance. "Have I got everything right?"

"Right on the nose, Counselor."

He nodded. "Well, in terms of logistics, it's no problem, but I think we haven't discussed how we're going to present this to the world at large."

She reared back. "Present what?"

"You living in my house, to start," he said without hesitation.

She frowned. "Do you need to clear it with someone? I'm sorry—I didn't even ask. I'm assuming you're still single, but maybe you're not?"

He shook his head hard. "Yes, still single. But this isn't Atlanta, Alicia. Around here, people will notice if I have a woman living in my house. People will notice, and people will talk."

"Is gossip a problem for you?" she asked, trying to keep the note of challenge from her tone, but failing.

"Not a problem, per se, but it's not going to go unnoticed." He smiled at her wanly. "You forget how it is in small towns. Everybody's business is everybody's business. So, for the sake of saving ourselves a whole lot of explaining and for providing you with cover for being here, I suggest we let people think we're a couple."

This time, Alicia pulled back. "A couple?"

"Together."

"Together?"

He sighed. "Alicia, I'm not saying it has to be the reality, but I think we should…"

"Put on an act?"

"…let people believe what they want to believe," he finished. "Trust me—it would be so much easier to deal with the Nosy Nellies if we let them think we're romantically involved."

"Won't we be inviting even more questions?"

He shook his head. "Relationships they understand. We might get some blowback about living together after so little time together, but only from a few of the holier of the holy rollers. Trust me—you don't want to try to explain a one-night stand while celebrating the arrest and arraignment of the county's most infamous criminal, then us going our separate ways only to discover you're pregnant. Add in the bit about how I've got somebody trying to scare me away from even sitting in on this case, and it's a whole lot of talking on our part." He shrugged. "I say let them draw their conclusions and do their talking on their own."

"Well, when you put it in those terms…"

He inclined his head to her. "Exactly. Much easier to say we met when you were here and started dating long-distance. You've got time off and have come down to stay with me. That's all there is to it."

She sat back and eyed him closely. "For a guy who spent his life trying to ferret out the truth, you're awfully good at the subterfuge."

He chuckled. "The company I keep," he answered brusquely. "Now, I know this may be an unwelcome question, but are you hungry?"

"Starving, but I don't think I could manage much more than toast," she said with a tired smile.

"Toast I can handle." He jerked his head toward the kitchen and rose from the couch. "Come on—let's get something in your stomach and we can talk some more about what's really brought you here."

Alicia laughed, scrambling up from the sofa as he led the way to the kitchen. "There's no subterfuge with me, Counselor. I'll tell you straight up everything I know."

He stopped in the kitchen and surveyed his surroundings. Running a hand over the top of his head down the back of his neck, he snuck a peek at her before glancing at the fridge. "I can handle the toast, but will it bother you if I make myself something to eat?"

She wrinkled her nose. "This is your house, Harry. You don't need my permission to make yourself a meal. If I can't handle it, I'll leave the room."

He gestured toward her stomach. "I don't want to do anything to set off any kind of adverse reaction."

"Okay, well, can you survive on sandwiches for a

while?" she asked. "It's mainly cooking smells getting to me right now. I can stomach the scent of toast, but any kind of meat cooking is a no go… It sort of hits me wrong."

"I love a good sandwich." He nodded toward the kitchen table, where they'd sat a few nights before. "Make yourself comfortable."

Alicia watched as he moved from the refrigerator to the counter, reaching easily into drawers and cabinets for whatever he needed to construct what looked to be a sandwich straight out of a cartoon. "Wow, you don't mess around."

He slid a plate with two slices of dry wheat toast in front of her. "Butter? Jam?"

"No, thank you. Dry is best right now."

He brought two more bottles of water over to the table, then carried his thick sandwich over to join her. He sat across from her as if poised to spring up if necessary. "Is this okay?"

She smiled. "Harry, you don't need to walk on eggshells. I'll get through this, and so will you."

He smiled back at her, then picked up half of the monster sandwich he'd built. She watched his teeth flash white before they sank into the bread. But the moment he started to chew, the quiet of the kitchen was obliterated by the smash of glass and the soft whoosh of a fire igniting.

Harry and Alicia both leaped from the table and ran toward the living room. A cool breeze blew through a broken window. A glass Mason jar lay on its side, spilling liquid onto the hardwood floor, and about a foot away, a scrap of flaming cloth blazed too close to the curtains for comfort.

Chapter Eight

Harry's first instinct was to act, not to think. He ran into the living room, carefully jumped over the puddle spreading across his floor and stomped on the flaming rag as the fire licked at the bottom of the sheer curtains his sister had insisted he needed.

"Harry, stop," Alicia shouted, but he couldn't.

Cold air poured in through the broken window, but his blood ran hot. Thankfully, he hadn't yet taken off his shoes. The soles heated and the leather flexed as he stomped on the rag.

"Are you crazy?" Alicia demanded. "You're going to catch your pants on fire. Get out of there."

Harry kept his gaze fixed on the charred bit of rag he'd stomped to pieces, then yanked the curtains up to make sure they hadn't caught a spark.

"I think I got it out," he called back to her.

"There's a river of gasoline flowing toward you, and if you don't get away from the window, I'm gonna tackle you," she warned him.

He looked up and saw her poised inside the living room, her arms spread as she crouched, ready to launch herself at him.

"No need for tackling," he assured her.

"Be careful—it's spreading," she ordered.

He eyed the liquid spilling from the heavy jar. The pool was indeed spreading, but the flow ran straight in his direction. Damn this old house for not having level floors, he thought as he dragged the rag away from the encroaching liquid with his foot. Not taking his eyes off the gasoline, he asked, "Am I missing anything? Is it out?"

"Yes, you idiot. It's out."

He barked a laugh. "Tell me how you really feel about me," he joked as he stepped off the wad of incinerated fabric and moved back toward her.

"Someone threw a Molotov cocktail through your front window and you want to make jokes?"

Her sharp tone caught his attention. He stopped in front of her and placed both hands on her upper arms, drawing her up to her full height. "Sorry. Defense mechanism," he admitted gruffly. "My mother always said I tend to get flippant when I'm freaking out."

She stared back at him. He liked her height. Loved looking her straight in the eye and knowing she could meet him head-on in every way.

"Are you freaking out?"

"Someone threw a really bad Molotov cocktail through my front window." He gave her a wry half smile. "Safe to assume I'm freaking out."

"But you charged right in there and put it out," she countered. "With your feet."

"I'm wearing shoes."

She sighed, and he felt her entire body sag. "Well, I guess we should be okay as long as we don't light any matches."

He nodded, still holding her gaze. "Right. We're okay."

Alicia pulled back enough to peer around him at the mess. "We can go on believing we're not dealing with professionals."

"How do you figure?"

"Someone who knew what they were doing would have made it impossible for the wicking to come out. We got lucky."

He opted not to point out her choice of pronoun and simply nodded. "We did. Thank God for ineptitude." He gave her arms a gentle rub, then steered her back to the hall. "Would you call Ben for me?"

Giving him the side-eye, she asked, "What are you going to do?"

He nodded toward the kitchen. "Neither of us need to be standing by those fumes, broken window or not." He moved past her and went to the door to the garage. "I'm going to see what I have to soak up some of the kerosene, then find something to cover the window, otherwise it's going to get pretty chilly in here pretty fast."

"We need the ventilation," she said.

He stepped down into the garage he'd converted into a home gym. "Then we'll get it cleaned up."

"I don't suppose you have a cat," she said from too close behind him.

He whirled to find her standing in the open doorway. "A cat?" He shook his head. "No."

"Too bad, because I think you need kitty litter to tackle this spill." She held up her cell phone. "I'll ask Ben to pick some up on his way over."

He hesitated, then spoke his greatest worry aloud. "Staying here isn't the best idea for you."

Her spine stiffened. "Don't try to shield me. I'm no delicate flower for you to protect. I can take you out about nine different ways before I even have to reach for my gun."

"I believe you, but circumstances being what they are—"

"I don't run from danger—I run to it," she continued.

"I don't want you endangered on my account," he insisted.

"Tough."

The simple, somewhat adolescent response would have made him laugh if he weren't so damn frustrated and worried. Still, he kept his cool. Like he would a hostile witness, he needed to lead her to the conclusion he wanted her to make. "Again, circumstances, Alicia."

"I make my own decisions."

"Yes, but you're making them for two now," he pointed out.

"You can do whatever you want to do," she snapped back.

Her knee-jerk reaction and momentary oblivion startled a sharp laugh out of him. He walked back toward her, holding her belligerent stare every inch of the way. "I wasn't talking about you and me. I meant you and the baby."

Hectic color rose in her cheeks, and she shook her head hard as if she could dismiss his concerns with simple negation. "It doesn't matter. I'm not going anywhere," she said, thrusting her chin up as she crossed her arms over her chest.

He studied her for a moment, but rather than argue about it, he gave in. "All right. Then call Ben for me, will you? Tell him we need another damn hazmat cleanup."

Deputy Mike Schaeffer caught the call. A tall, borderline-gangly guy with an easy smile and good old-fashioned Southern manners, he'd shown up with the requested hazmat kit and an enormous bag of cat litter.

"It really is the best thing, but you have to get the kind with clay in it," he explained as he dumped the litter directly onto the kerosene. "The problem is, takes forever to get the smell out. Of the kerosene, I mean." He shook his head, a rueful smile on his lips. "My cousin knocked over a heater at our hunting cabin, and I swear we had to air the place out for weeks."

Harry made an unintelligible grunt in response. Which wasn't fair. He liked Mike. The guy was a good cop, down-to-earth and thorough. Qualities Harry usually appreciated. But his front window was broken and the cool December air was gushing in. Harry was damn tired of people taking out their petty complaints about his job on his house.

They wanted him to quit the case. What they failed to realize was, with or without him, Samuel Coulter's day in court was coming. He'd spoken to Marcus Zeller, the federal prosecutor who'd serve as first chair on the case, the day before and filled him in on what was happening. Zeller assured him he was needed on the case, and if he wasn't put off by what he termed *pregame theatrics*, he still wanted Harry on the litigation.

Rather than making him want to give up his second-chair position, these assaults made him want to get Coulter to court even faster. He longed to be there to help US Attorney Zeller nail the smuggler to a wall. He needed to show these thugs he wasn't afraid of them.

Then, when everything was said and done, he could go back to prosecuting domestic disturbances, property damage issues, and small-time drug peddlers spread through the backwoods of Georgia as thick on the ground as kudzu. He'd prosecute people who keyed cars and slashed tires for criminal mischief. But this stuff—the shots taken at his house and now this homemade hand grenade—it elevated things to terroristic threatening levels.

A Molotov cocktail, he thought, incredulous. Scrubbing a hand over his face, he searched for something to say to the young deputy who was working so hard to help with the mess in the living room. "Not the best time of year for airing things out," he managed at last.

"No, sir," Mike responded affably. "It's a chilly one tonight."

The deputy rocked back and pursed his lips as he surveyed the mess they'd spread upon mess. Rubbing the back of his neck, Mike shrugged one shoulder. "I guess you can try some lemon. My mama always said it was best for neutralizing odors. But you might wanna check the internet first. I'm not exactly sure what the best solution might be. Citrus can be awful acidic, you know."

Harry was almost overtaken by the urge to smile at the remark, but he held back. He appreciated the young man's need to be helpful. Instead, he clapped the deputy on the shoulder as they took in the clumps of granulated litter now covering his living-room floor. "Thanks, Mike. You went above and beyond, and I appreciate it."

"It was no big deal," Mike said with a shrug. "A quick run into the Stop & Shop on my way over. Sheriff should be here shortly."

"Okay. Yeah, I guess I shouldn't have called him

into this. You have it well in hand," he said to the deputy.

Mike only chuckled. "I know the sheriff, and I can tell you he wants to be in on this."

No sooner were the words out than there was a sharp rap on the front door. As usual, Ben let himself in after waiting only a moment. Stopping dead in the middle of the entrance, the sheriff stared at the two of them, amazed disbelief written all over his face. "A Molotov cocktail? Are you kidding me?"

As if on cue, Alicia stepped out of the kitchen, where he'd left her propped up against the counter, snacking on a sleeve of saltines. "Not a very good one. They used a canning jar but no lid or anything to hold the fabric in place to ignite the fuel."

"Thank God for small favors," Ben replied.

"And idiotic assassins," Alicia added dryly. When both Ben and Harry swung their heads around altogether, she shrugged and asked, "Too soon?"

"Yes," Harry replied tersely.

"Got it." Alicia nodded. "I'll stow the cop humor until later."

Ben smiled and shook his head. "I've got a couple good ones in mind. Remind me later, when Harry finds his sense of humor again."

"I'm ready to give my statement," Harry snapped.

Not missing a beat, Ben pulled his trusty notebook and pen out of the back pocket of his jeans and nodded toward the kitchen. "We'll step in there so we can stay out of the fumes." He glanced over at the living room. "Thanks for running interference on the hazmat, Mike," he said with a nod to his deputy. "I called the fire chief, and he said litter was the right thing to use." Shifting his attention back to Harry, he added, "He also said to call them if we want them to come out and take a look."

"Fire's out," Harry said flatly. "Let's get this over with."

While Mike gathered his gear in the living room, Harry pulled out his wallet and extracted a twenty. "Here." When the deputy tried to wave him off, he shook his head. "For the litter. Thank you."

"The least I could do," Mike responded, taking the bill with a nod. "Night."

After seeing Mike out, Harry joined Alicia and Ben in the kitchen. They took the same seats at the table they'd claimed a few nights before. The second they were settled, Harry began to talk without prompting.

"Alicia and I were here in the kitchen talking when we heard something come through the window. When we ran in there, I saw the jar and make-shift wick had separated, so I extinguished the fire by stepping on it. The fire didn't spread to anything else, but now I have a living room soaked with kerosene."

"I'm not going to bother asking you if you have any ideas who might've done this," Ben murmured as he made notes on the page. "Can you give me the time frame?"

Harry and Alicia exchanged a look as they both scrambled to pinpoint the sequence of events on a clock. "I think I got here at about six thirty," she said slowly.

Harry nodded. "We talked for a while, and then I was going to make something to eat," he continued. "I'm pretty sure the clock on the stove showed after seven when I got up."

Alicia shrugged and nodded. "It's coming on eight, so it couldn't have been after seven."

Ben's head swiveled as he switched his gaze back and forth. "Narrows it down some." He flipped his notebook shut, placed his hands on the table in front of him and zoomed in on Alicia. "Didn't expect to see you back in town so soon," he said in a conversational tone. "Did you come to sing Christmas carols this time?"

"She came to see me," Harry said, hoping to put the kibosh on any teasing. He wasn't in the mood for games.

His strident tone did the trick. Ben sat up straighter and shifted the full force of his attention to him. "I'd assumed as much."

Their eyes met and held. It was all Harry could do to resist shifting under the sheriff's unblinking gaze, but he held it together. Barely. Ben glanced over at Alicia, saving him from having to come up with a better story than the "we're together" plan they'd settled on minutes before the night went all to hell.

Thankfully, Alicia was better at this stuff. She

met Ben's perusal with a smirky smile, daring the sheriff to pry. When the tension stretched so taut Harry thought he might have to spill the whole story to exonerate himself, she spoke.

"We're together."

Harry blinked, surprised to hear their plan spoken aloud and with such simplicity it made any further probing seem like an overreach.

"Ah," Ben said. He had the grace to nod as if he hadn't put one and one together on his own, then tapped the top of his notepad. "I, uh, figured something was going on."

"You're so smart," Alicia cooed, letting her smirk stretch into a teasing smile.

Ben smiled back, but slid his attention back to Harry so quickly he wasn't able to plaster one on in time. The sharp glint in the sheriff's eyes said he hadn't missed the moment of hesitation, but he was merciful enough to let the lack of deeper explanation slide.

"Marlee will be glad to hear it. Since Simon and Lori are dating, she seems determined to see everyone she knows paired up," Ben said dryly.

"Of course. No one loves love as much as a lover," Alicia said, her smile so wide Harry felt his own cheeks ache.

Harry wondered if she realized she'd thrown the *L* word out there like a live grenade. Still, he needed to get himself together. Pull his weight. If they were going to make the citizens of Pine Bluff believe there was something going on between them, there was no better place to start than with the county's top cop.

"We, uh, got to know each other when she was here a couple months ago," Harry said, warming up slowly.

"Obviously," Alicia said with a laugh.

She reached over and put her hand over his, but Harry got the feeling she was trying to quell him rather than show affection. He must be worse at this than he thought.

"We've talked some, but with the reorg at work, I haven't had a chance to get back to Pine Bluff until the other night."

Harry couldn't help but stare at her. He could only hope his admiration was coming across as something more romantic than appreciating her skill at embroidering the truth. Other than the announcement of their "together-ness," she hadn't lied. Judging by the size of the suitcase he'd rolled into the guest room, they actually would be together for the foreseeable future. How other people defined the word wasn't their problem, was it?

No. Their problem was something far more sinister than whether he and the DEA agent who'd brought Samuel Coulter down had something going on.

"Back to this thing tonight," Harry said, hoping to refocus the conversation. "I think we can all agree this is an escalation."

Ben and Alicia both nodded. "Undoubtedly," the sheriff said.

"And not a tactic we'd expect anyone from around these parts to employ," Harry continued.

"Which is why I came here tonight," Alicia interrupted.

Caught off guard, Harry's head swiveled in time with Ben's.

"Oh?" The sheriff slipped open the notepad again. "What have you found?"

Something about the way Ben asked the question clued Harry in. Ben knew Alicia was looking into the threats against him. She must have talked to the sheriff in the days since she'd left Pine Bluff, but she hadn't bothered to call him. A surge of jealous anger sliced through him, but he bit the inside of his cheek to keep from saying anything.

"I put out feelers about the groups you identified and a couple more I pulled from our own database, but couldn't come up with anything tying them directly to Coulter or that would give me a reason why they'd be interested in his case."

"Yeah, I've been coming up empty too," Ben admitted. "We have a lead involving a motorcycle club called The Outriders, but nothing concrete on them yet."

"A couple of their members were at Dusty's Barbecue at the exact same time all four of my tires were slashed."

Her head whipped around. "Your tires were slashed?"

Harry nodded, a grim frown tugging at his mouth. "Yes. Again. While I was eating dinner last night."

"But no one saw those guys move," Ben pointed out. "I questioned them myself, then asked everyone who was there if they'd seen either of them budge from their table, and came up empty."

"Maybe they messaged some friends," Harry tossed out.

Ben shrugged. "It's possible, but even if they said, *Hey, Harry Hayes is here, come and slash his tires!* we wouldn't be much closer to the root of the problem. I can't help going back around to thinking there's a local connection. Your guy at the US Attorney's Office hasn't had any trouble like this."

She shook her head. "Nothing out of the ordinary. I agree with you, Ben. Someone has taken up Coulter's cause, and they're making it personal with Harry."

The sheriff found his gaze again. "I don't suppose you'd consider—"

Harry didn't let him finish. "No. I'm not backing off."

"I already tried," Alicia said with a wry smirk.

"Of course you have," Ben answered smoothly. He blew out a breath and tapped his pen on the pad. "So you're coming up empty too?"

"I didn't say I came up empty," Alicia corrected, smooth as silk.

This time, when both men focused on her, she looked at Harry. "Did you know Ben spent a good deal of time undercover for the agency? He was what some people call an embedded asset."

Across the table, Ben sat up straighter. "What are you getting at?"

Alicia wet her lips before answering. "We have another agent working deep with The Disciples. It seems they picked up a couple of former Southeast members."

Ben went completely still but said nothing, so Harry waded in. "Southeast members?"

"A gang based out of Southeast Atlanta. Called themselves SEATL. They ran a lot of crystal meth," she explained. To Ben she said, "I listened to some audio our operative gathered and there's talk of getting the old gang back together again. One of the guys they mentioned was Anton Brooks."

"Anton?" Ben repeated, as if mesmerized by the name.

"Who is Anton Brooks?" Harry asked, tired of being on the outside of this conversation looking in.

At last, Ben snapped out of his trance. "Anton Brooks is the younger brother of Andre Brooks…my best friend growing up. He's dead. Andre, I mean," he said gruffly.

"I'm sorry," Harry said, the response automatic, but genuine.

"Andre was the right-hand man to SEATL's leader, Ivan Jones," Alicia explained. She looked at him as if the name should mean something to him. Which it didn't. But it clearly meant something to Ben.

"Jones is dead too," he said flatly.

She nodded. "Yes. But you know there's always someone willing to step in."

"You're telling me Anton Brooks is trying to revive the operation?" Ben pressed, leaning forward.

Alicia nodded. "Rumor has it, he was handpicked by Ivan's partner before he died."

"Ivan or the business partner?" Harry interrupted, still trying to grab the tread of the conversation.

Alicia shrugged. "Well, they're both dead, but his business partner was the one to pick him. This is where it gets interesting," she said, her eyes sharp. "You might not know Ivan Jones, but I bet you've heard of his partner, Harry. He was an attorney named Jared Baker."

"Jared Baker?" He swung his gaze to Ben, who looked about as shocked and confused as Harry felt. "He was the guy tied to all the murders set up to look like suicide. Clint Young, Bo Abernathy—"

"And Marlee's brother, Jeff," Ben finished for him. Pushing up from his chair, the sheriff ran a hand across the back of his neck. "So Baker bestowed little Anton," he murmured. "But I can't imagine any of the other players are going to let him waltz in and take back what they gobbled up of Ivan's empire."

"Seems unlikely, doesn't it?" Alicia said, watching him warily. "But it looks like they may have a new moneyman. Someone with enough clout to make them all play nice together. At least for the moment."

"Any idea who?"

"Nothing for certain," Alicia hedged. "But I did come across something interesting when looking into Baker."

"What?" Harry asked, making a mental note to make her stitch this all together for him the minute Ben left.

"I was poking around to see who some of his old clients were, and guess whose name I came across?"

Harry's stomach sank and his heart rate kicked into overdrive. "No."

She nodded, unwilling to let him cling to his oblivion for more than a minute. "Yes. It appears Baker was the attorney of record when Samuel Coulter purchased a large parcel of timberland located in Masters County, Georgia."

Chapter Nine

Alicia stood in line at the bakery the next morning, bleary-eyed and her stomach rumbling at the sight of all the pastries in the case. Harry had left a note welcoming her to help herself to whatever she'd like, but she still wasn't feeling comfortable enough to make a mess in his kitchen. The previous night had proved to be enough of a mess for both of them.

After Ben left, they had sat at the table nibbling on crackers and cheese and talking about, well, everything. Harry filled her in on the spate of suicide-murders in Masters County in the previous year, all of which were connected to Attorney Jared Baker and the methamphetamine trade in the area.

She filled Harry in on Ivan Jones and the bounty the gang leader had put on Ben's head, even though the man had been behind bars. With his cover blown and a price on his head, the DEA considered Ben more of a liability than an asset. The biggest bust of his career had also ended up costing Ben his job and his home. No place in Atlanta was safe for him.

He'd had to leave, which was why he ended up taking the job as sheriff of Masters County.

Sipping from bottles of water, they had sat in the quiet. Alicia marveled at the realization that their lives had been unknowingly and loosely intertwined for many months before they'd actually laid eyes on one another. When she could no longer stifle her yawns, he insisted she go to bed and get her rest. By the time she woke, he'd already left for work. And despite the note written in neat block letters and left on the kitchen table, she'd wager he hadn't made himself breakfast. There were no dishes in the sink or even a crumb on the counter. He was likely afraid to light the gas stove. The house still reeked of kerosene.

The kitchen window had been cracked about an inch, letting in a steady stream of cool air, but without opening another to create a cross draft, it was doing nothing to help disperse the smell. Alicia had peeled back the plastic on the broken window enough to allow it to vent a bit in hopes of encouraging dissipation. Then she'd headed for the bakery she remembered had the best coffee in town.

Unfortunately, the real stuff was off her menu now, but she was still counting on decaf and self-delusion to rev her system. And a pastry. A body needed fuel, after all.

As she walked the two blocks to the business district, she took the time to survey her surroundings more carefully. She found it easier to brainstorm when she had the setting fixed firmly in her mind.

Who was behind these assaults on Harry's property? She couldn't imagine anyone hating him enough to do these things. Verbal threats, sure. And maybe the envelope thing, she conceded. But shooting up a man's house was something entirely different. But the failed Molotov cocktail? Whoever was doing this had gone a bridge too far. This wasn't someone local. Or not entirely. But there had to be some locals involved somehow, didn't there? Perhaps Coulter had sunk his roots deeper into Masters County than anyone realized.

If there was anyone local involved, there was no better course of action in a small town than putting one's ear to the ground. She remembered Brewster's Bakery with its pink awning from her previous stay in the area. It and the neon-lit Daisy Drive-In were the spots where locals congregated. Her stomach growled, and though she considered drinking decaf a step above drinking a brown crayon melted in hot water, she saw no better place to start her day than the bakery.

A bell above the door announced her arrival. As she stepped into the sugar-scented warmth of the café, she glanced around, hoping to spot a familiar face seated at one of the small tables. Sadly, she came up empty. Not a big surprise. She didn't know many people in Pine Bluff, and most of them were either attached to the sheriff's department or the local attorneys. All people who'd likely been at their desks for a couple of hours.

When she stepped up to the counter, she smiled engagingly at the woman with salt-and-pepper hair standing poised to take her order.

"Good morning," Alicia said briskly but with what she hoped was a friendly smile. "I'd like a decaf Americano, and one of those chocolate croissants."

The woman nodded and spun away to prepare her order. Seconds later, a paper cup and a white bakery bag appeared on the counter, and the woman started punching numbers into the cash register.

"Coffee and croissant comes to six forty-nine."

Alicia glanced over her shoulder at the tables where people were drinking their coffee from oversize mugs and eating off of mismatched china plates with real silverware. "Oh, I'm sorry. I should've said it was for here."

The older woman paused, her expression neutral but unwavering. "Oh, well, you're welcome to eat here if you'd like. Six forty-nine," she repeated.

Alicia raised her eyebrows as she handed over her debit card. The woman swiped it, punched in the amount of the charge and waited for the ancient printer to spool out a receipt.

Desperate to establish some rapport, Alicia nodded to the outdated credit-card machine. "Still swiping, huh?" The other woman looked up at her, the bland expression she wore hardening. A moment too late, she realized the woman probably found her comment insulting. "I mean, most places have a chip reader or even one of those scanners where you tap the card…"

She trailed off as the woman yanked her receipt from the machine and pushed it across the counter.

"Yes, well, this one works fine, and when I need a new one, I'll get a new one. Thank you. Have a nice day," the woman responded curtly.

She leaned to her left and peered at the customer behind Alicia in case she hadn't gotten the hint. Alicia stepped away, and the woman behind the counter smiled so broadly it transformed her entire face. "Good morning, Carolee. I wasn't expecting to see you in here. What can I do for you today?"

Taking her cup and to-go bag, Alicia moved to an open table nestled against the far wall. From there, she watched people come and go from the busy bakery.

Almost everyone stopped to chat with at least one or two people on the way in or out. The place seemed to be humming. High on the exchange of information as much as the sugar, she suspected. Unfortunately, the mishmash of soft-spoken Southern accents made it hard to pick out any particular tidbits.

She took a sulky sip of her coffee and tore the corner of her croissant into bite-size pieces, arranging them on top of the sheet of wax paper it came wrapped in. She couldn't take her eyes off the woman who'd taken her order. She was speaking to an immaculately dressed blonde woman who looked like she'd never touched a doughnut in her life.

Alicia popped a bite of buttery pastry into her mouth and tried to pick apart the sudden surge of resentment she felt as she watched the easy exchange between the two women. She slumped lower in her seat and watched them through narrowed eyes when a familiar voice interrupted her ruminations.

"Hello, Alicia."

Sitting up straighter, she jerked her head up to find Marlee Masters beaming down at her.

"Ben told me you were back in town."

Alicia dropped the hunk of croissant she was smashing between her thumb and forefinger and quickly wiped her hand on a paper napkin from the dispenser on the table. "Oh, yes. Hello. Nice to see you again."

Marlee's smile widened as she waved to someone across the room. "May I?" she asked, gesturing to the empty seat across from her.

"Please."

"I snuck away from the office. I swear, some days it's a meeting about a meeting about when to schedule a meeting to have a meeting," she said with a laugh. She nodded her head toward the woman at the counter. "Over there's my mama. Carolee Masters," she added. "She wanted to come down here to order some pastries for bridge club, and had gone by the house to talk to Daddy, so I volunteered to be her chauffeur."

"I thought you said you were in meetings," Alicia pointed out.

Marlee shook her head. "No, I said today was all about meetings, but I didn't say I was participating in them. One of the perks as boss."

She said the last with such an engaging smile, Alicia couldn't help reciprocating. "It must be nice."

"I'll go back after I drop Mom off again," Marlee said, waving her hand dismissively. "But in the meantime—" She looked up and, as if on cue, the woman who had waited on Alicia so brusquely a few minutes before appeared beside the table.

She held a large cup and saucer, and a plate with what appeared to be a breakfast sandwich made out of a fluffy biscuit. "There you go, Miss Marlee," the woman practically cooed.

Marlee gazed openmouthed at the food.

"Thank you so much, Miss Camille. This is a treat."

"I made it with egg whites like your mama likes, so you don't have to feel guilty about anything."

"Thank you for looking out for me." Marlee managed to say the last bit without even a hint of sarcasm.

Alicia found herself staring at Marlee in shock. Wasn't she insulted about the implication of watching her weight? Apparently not.

Marlee simply smiled. "I'll see you at Tuesday night's Slim Session?" she asked, her voice sweet as honey.

The woman called Miss Camille pulled a face and

blushed. "I suppose I should come, but I have to tell you my weigh-in won't be any good. I've been sampling more of the wares than I should lately."

Marlee shook her head. "You know it's not all about what the scale says—it's about how we feel. If you'd like to attend, and you need support, we'll be there for you."

When the other woman walked away, Alicia looked at Marlee agog.

"Slim Sessions?"

Marlee chuckled. "The name is kind of a holdover from my mom's days, and we don't do the whole diet thing like they used to do where they eat nothing but a couple leaves of lettuce. I'm trying to help it to evolve into something more…holistic. Diet, exercise and generally what we're doing to make ourselves feel good these days. More of an all-around support group, I guess." She frowned as she picked up the layered breakfast biscuit. "We really do need to think of a better name," she murmured before taking a hefty bite.

"At least you got a plate," Alicia pointed out, gesturing from her crushed bag and wax-paper place mat to Marlee's plate, cup and saucer.

"Oh." Marlee's brows knit as she chewed, eyeing the bag and paper cup. "I think Mrs. Brewster assumes people who are not from here are passing through." She hesitated for a moment. "I'd tell you not to take it personally, but in truth, I think she means it to be personal."

Marlee's candor made Alicia laugh out loud. The sound drew the attention of the few people seated around them, but Alicia didn't care. There were worse things than being seen laughing and enjoying breakfast with the town's biggest mogul.

"I was hoping to put my ear to the ground and pick up some gossip while I was here, but it doesn't look like I'll have much luck," Alicia said, wrinkling her nose.

Marlee chewed thoughtfully, then took a sip from the enormous mug. "Small towns can be tough to crack."

"An understatement," Alicia said wryly.

"No doubt." Marlee chuckled. "But I understand why people are wary. Pine Bluff is small, but we've had a lot of trouble in the past few years. More trouble than any town this size should. Right now, people are stuck in some kind of nostalgia loop." She set her biscuit back down and pulled a paper napkin from the dispenser to wipe her fingers. "There's a whole contingent of them who think we were living in a damn Norman Rockwell painting before all this 'trouble,'" she said, using air quotes, "came to town. But I grew up here, and I can tell you this was no paradise before."

"This is Georgia, not Utopia," Alicia said with a nod.

"Exactly. Ben tells me you're looking into drawing some connection between the group who was after him in Atlanta and whoever's doing these things to Harry," Marlee said, lacing her fingers together and leaning in as she spoke softly. "I want you to know I will help in whatever way I can."

Alicia was smart enough to know this was no small offer. Marlee was a Masters of Masters County. She ran the timber company founded by her great-great-grandfather. The company was the largest employer in the area, which made Marlee a powerful woman. If she pledged her support, it wasn't a token gesture.

"I appreciate the offer," Alicia said sincerely. "And I want you to know I always thought Ben had been treated very unfairly by the agency. They should have done more for him. They should've found a way to protect their own."

Marlee nodded. "I agree. But I'm also glad they didn't, otherwise he never would've landed here."

"Things have a way of working out, regardless of what we plan," Alicia said, almost to herself.

"They do indeed." Marlee sat up straight again, picked up her sandwich and bit into it. "Oh!" she said through stuffed cheeks. Cupping a hand over her mouth, she continued to speak. "Sorry. I was thinking we need Lori. Lori will help," she said, her voice garbled.

"I'll take any help I can get, but why wouldn't people talk to Lori? She's from here too," she pointed out.

Marlee nodded vigorously as she chewed, then swallowed hard. With another slurp of her latte, she swiped the napkin from her lap and wiped her mouth.

"But she's the law. Some people get hung up on the badge."

"I see." Alicia popped another bite of croissant into her mouth and chewed slowly. If some locals wouldn't talk around Lori because she was a cop, then surely others would clam up around Marlee since she likely held the keys to their livelihoods, but maybe between the three of them…

Marlee wiped her mouth again, then nodded. "Don't you worry. Between Lori and me, you'll have an in about anywhere you want around here. And between the three of us, surely we can hear something."

"You read my mind." Marlee laughed, but Alicia was not entirely convinced. "What makes you think we can get any further than Ben has gotten?"

Marlee snorted. "Listen, I love the man, so I'm admittedly not the most objective person when it comes to him, but I can tell you this—people like Ben, but he's an outsider." She shrugged. "They might start letting him in here and there, but he's never going to have the network of information someone who is born and raised here would have. Heck, even Mike Schaeffer has an advantage on him," she said, referring to one of Ben's deputies.

"I see," she repeated.

"Don't worry—he knows it," Marlee said, picking a bit of the biscuit off and lobbing it into her mouth. "I like to tease him and say he keeps me around because I'm his golden ticket."

Alicia eyed the radiant blonde seated across from

her and laughed. "I'm pretty sure that's not why he keeps you around. I've never seen a man more smitten."

A peachy blush colored Marlee's cheeks. "Well, the feeling is entirely mutual, in case you were wondering," she said with a pointed look.

"I wasn't wondering. It's crystal clear."

"Marlee, honey," her mother called from across the room. "Come on—I need to get back to your daddy."

Marlee glanced mournfully down at the remainder of the breakfast biscuit and tossed her paper napkin on the table. "Coming, Mama." She rose, lifting her coffee cup in one fluid motion. "Let me get a to-go cup for my latte."

Carolee Masters shook her head when she spotted her daughter's abandoned plate. "Marlee, you know how it is with biscuits—two minutes on the lips and forever on the hips."

"Well, now, Mama, you know we don't think about food in those terms anymore," Marlee said with a toss of her golden hair. "Food is fuel. It's all about making the right choices at the right time. And I can tell you at this very moment my belly was craving a biscuit, and I am not gonna apologize to my hips."

Alicia fought the urge to applaud. She watched as Marlee sashayed up to the counter and handed over her unfinished coffee to be poured into a paper cup. When her mother approached, Marlee leaned in and kissed her cheek. Clearly there were no hard feelings generated by their exchange.

Alicia watched heads swivel as the Masters women made their way to the door, calling out goodbyes and wishing various people nice days and asking to be remembered to other people as they passed.

When the bell above the door jingled, she stared down at the remnants of the bacon-and-egg biscuit. Probably what she should have ordered. She was pregnant. She needed to start eating like a grown-up, not a teenager, she admonished herself. More protein. Maybe some leafy greens, she thought, barely suppressing a shudder.

Miss Camille appeared at her table to clear Marlee's place. "Can I get you a top-off on your coffee, sugar?" she asked in a markedly friendlier manner.

Alicia glanced down at the plastic dome of the coffee cup and figured more decaf couldn't hurt. "Yes, please. I'm drinking decaf."

"Be right back," Camille Brewster replied. Then she bustled away.

Alicia managed a couple more bites of croissant and a sip of her now lukewarm coffee. Even though the coffee tasted the same as regular, she missed the kick of caffeine. The combination of a lack of stimulant and what the doctor termed early-pregnancy exhaustion was going to be crippling.

Ms. Brewster startled her from her thoughts when she placed the cup and saucer down on the table with a clatter. Alicia stared, her eyes fixed on the heavy porcelain cup. "Thank you," she managed. "What do I owe you?"

The older woman simply shook her head. "Refills are on the house."

Alicia watched in astonishment as the woman who'd barely acknowledged her a short time before made her way back to the counter.

Determined to make a good impression, Alicia cleaned up scraps of her croissant and brushed every last crumb into the bag she'd revived. All in all, not a bad trip to the bakery, even if she didn't overhear anything about Harry's tormentors. She was more than happy to take advantage of Marlee's generous offer to help her break through some of the small-town barriers, but would also take heed not to be fooled into thinking she belonged because people didn't treat her like a stranger. Marlee's words about Ben and his ability to fit into Pine Bluff society resonated with her.

As a military kid, Alicia had been an outsider her entire life, moving from post to post, never making deep, decades-long friendships. Having gone through life without forming attachments had served her well when she went to work for the agency. She hadn't always been partnered with the most forward-thinking people, nor had some of her bosses been as enthusiastic about having her in their ranks as one would hope. Bronson was a good example. But she'd survived others like him, and she would figure out a way to carry on. She would be the one in control of her destiny with the agency.

She sipped until she'd depleted the second cup of coffee. When she was done, she gathered the paper goods as well as her cup and saucer and carried them back to the counter.

"Oh, let me get those," Camille said, snatching the bag from Alicia's hand, looking slightly abashed. She put the cup and saucer into a black tub behind her. "Everything okay, I hope?"

"Everything was delicious, thank you." Alicia hesitated for a moment, then decided if she was going to make a go of her time here in Pine Bluff, she needed to go all in. "Mrs. Brewster, I don't suppose you could tell me what it is Harry Hayes prefers or how he takes his coffee?"

Camille Brewster's eyebrows rose almost to her hairline. "Harry Hayes?"

Alicia nodded and did her best to look bashful. She wasn't sure if she was pulling it off, given the look of consternation on Mrs. Brewster's face. "Yes. You see, I'm staying with him and I'd like to take him something at the office, but I wasn't sure what he prefers."

"Staying with him?" Camille Brewster repeated.

Alicia fought the urge to smile. She knew the information would go out on the wire before the door closed behind her. "Yes."

The confirmation seemed to snap the other woman from her trance. "Oh, well, Harry doesn't like anything particularly fancy. A doughnut every once in a while. Glazed or twist, usually, but sometimes he goes for the cream-filled."

"Great. I'll take one of each. And a coffee," she added. "Whatever he usually orders."

The woman looked at her blankly for a moment. "Coffee? Harry doesn't drink coffee."

Alicia gaped at the woman, struck silent for a moment. "Doesn't drink coffee?"

The other woman laughed. "I know, right?" She shook her head. "Occasionally, he'll buy a bottle of orange juice, but mostly I think he sticks to water."

Alicia goggled at the woman. "No caffeine at all?"

Camille Brewster's lips drew tight, and for a moment Alicia thought she might've stepped over the line, but then she shook her head in bewildered dismay. "No. None. I honestly don't know how the man makes it through the day."

Chapter Ten

Harry walked into his office to find the place deserted and a fat stack of mail piled at the center of his blotter. His ADA, Danielle, was likely across the hall talking to Julianne in the sheriff's department. The intern they'd hired from Albany State University, Layla, had mentioned running to the Piggly Wiggly for break-room supplies. Ever since the debacle with the envelope delivered to his house, he'd insisted he open his own mail. The last thing he wanted was for the people who worked for him to open anything dangerous or even questionable.

If someone was coming after him, they needed to keep him and him alone in their sights.

Sighing, he dropped his briefcase onto the desk and used the corner of it to push the pile around a bit. It looked like a mishmash of number-ten business envelopes and Christmas cards. There were a couple of larger manila envelopes. Dropping into his chair, he closed his eyes and gave himself a minute to process what had transpired in Judge Nichols's chambers.

At any other time, he would not have thought anything about a twenty-year-old kid getting busted for possession, but now every single drug-related incident in Masters County felt personal to him.

He'd been there when the DEA's methamphetamine raids had decimated the town. He'd been there when the power struggle resulting from those arrests led to a series of heartbreaking murders made to look like suicides. Then Samuel Coulter moved in and changed the face of it all. Wealthy and urbane, Coulter had been an object of curiosity, and yes, even admiration to some, when he first moved to Masters County. Judging from the gossip he heard around town, some of the women considered the man handsome, but Harry could only figure they'd never seen him up close and personal.

His own dealings with Coulter left him feeling cold inside. Like he'd swallowed an ice cube whole and it landed in the empty pit of his stomach and refused to melt.

The man was off. He'd seen it from the moment they met. But getting a hinky feeling about someone and being able to prosecute them for a crime heinous enough to put them away for a good long time were two very different things.

Earlier, he'd given Judge Nichols a brief rundown of all the incidents involving his property. Harry and the judge had worked closely for a number of years, and since his office was adjacent to the judge's chambers, he felt the man should be in the know. He also wanted someone in a trusted position, someone who wasn't law enforcement or had any personal vested interest in seeing Coulter convicted beyond a thirst for justice, to know what was happening.

In the event something should happen to Harry.

Judge Nichols, always a fair and patient man, had listened calmly, taken notes and assured Harry if the worst ever came to pass he would throw the full weight of his influence behind flushing out who was responsible for these misdeeds.

Harry had felt comforted for the five minutes it took to walk from Judge Nichols's chambers back to his own office.

The stack of mail had undone his sense of calm.

Pulling a letter opener from the center desk drawer, Harry leaned closer to the pile and began to shift it with the tip of the blade to survey the contents. The number-ten envelopes were likely simple correspondence from law firms in the area. He saw the logo from Wendell Wingate's firm, now run by his grandson Simon, printed on the corner of one. The names on the Christmas cards were all familiar to him. Mostly colleagues, but a few friends from college, and a couple of locals who knew the best way to get him was always at work rather than home.

He snared the edge of one envelope with the tip of the opener and pushed it from the pile. The sticker in the corner showed it was from Lourdes Cabrera. He had only seen Lori in passing since the night of the mystery powder scare, but the sight of the card made him smile. He pulled the envelope out of the stack and slit it open. Deputy Cabrera had sent him a Christmas card. Mailed it, even though they worked directly across the foyer from one another. He couldn't wait to prod Lori's boyfriend, Simon, about making her list.

When he removed the heavy card stock from the envelope, he saw it wasn't simply a card but an invitation. A tastefully designed holiday party invitation. He smiled at the sight of it. Elsewhere in the world, emails, texts and phone calls might be enough, but here in South Georgia, when a person was throwing a soiree of some import, paper invitations were still the done thing.

Harry rocked back in his seat smiling as he read the details. Lori may have mailed the invitation, but the holiday party was to be held at Simon's house. His eyebrows rose when he noted the date. It was set for this coming Saturday, which meant this had been thrown together at the very last minute…or he'd been an afterthought on the invitation list. The second notion made him frown. In the past few months, Harry had come to consider Simon, Ben and Lori some of his closest friends. He preferred to assume the party was arranged last minute, and not that he was on the B-list.

No sooner had the thought entered his mind than a text message buzzed on his phone. He extracted it from his suit pocket and read the screen. It was from Simon Wingate.

Did you get the invitation?

Harry smirked. The impatience was typical for Simon. Thumbs flying, he texted back.

Just opened it. Did you forget to mail mine in the first round?

The three dots appeared and Harry found himself partially holding his breath as he waited for his friend to reply.

This is the first round, Simon said in the first bubble. It's kind of a last-minute thing. I was going to text, but Lori wouldn't let me.

Harry snickered, but before he could reply, another bubble appeared.

Can you make it?

I don't see why not, he typed back.

The three dots appeared again, and then the answer to Harry's next question magically appeared.

And Alicia? Are you bringing her?

Apparently, he was expected to bring his guest. A flashback of hot, hungry kisses ignited in his mind. The last time he and Alicia had attended a party at Simon's house, the evening had not only ended with them tangled in the sheets, but also…a baby.

If she wants to come, he eventually typed.

There was a longer pause as the ellipses blinked on the screen. A larger text bubble appeared.

Good, because we're having this thing since Lori heard Alicia was back to stay for a bit and you two are together. I think she might have a girl crush on Alicia. Either way, any excuse for a party, right?

Harry chuckled, tickled by Simon's reasoning.

This way, you get to be the first people in town hosting a Christmas party.

May have crossed our minds, Simon replied. Another bubble appeared a moment later. See you Saturday.

Setting his phone aside, Harry decided to start in on the rest of the Christmas cards to see if they also had surprises in store. Alas, they were the usual assortment of family photo collages, winter landscapes or variations on jolly old St. Nick.

Next, he opened the correspondence from the law firms, unfolded the papers and gave them a quick scan before putting them in his outbox for his assistant to pick up and add to the appropriate files.

Only the two manila envelopes were left.

He prodded each one with the tip of the letter opener. One looked to be filled with paperwork and appeared to have been sent by the Prescott County district attorney. The other appeared to have some sort of item enclosed in a hard square, like a picture frame. The return address showed it was from his sister.

Curious as to why Sarah would be mailing something to his office rather than to the house, he slipped the package open and peered inside. There was a framed photo and a note. Harry smiled, expecting to see another artfully casual shot of his nephews romping in a park or rolling in the snow or some such thing.

He pulled the frame from the envelope and the folded sheet of paper covering the glass fluttered. He picked it up, but rather than his sister's hurried cursive, he saw a single typed sentence.

"Next time it won't be a rock."

He stared at the paper for a moment, willing his brain to absorb both the unexpected message and the import. As it was, all he could do was catalog the facts as he saw them. Plain white copier paper. Standard Courier font, no bigger than twelve point. A threat. Mailed from his sister's address.

"What the—"

He bit back the profanity and dropped the piece of paper atop the frame once again and grabbed the envelope. It was postmarked in Atlanta. Not mailed from his sister's address. It was a ploy. A way to get him to open the damn thing without a second thought.

He snatched the piece of paper from the frame and found himself staring down at a photograph of

Samuel Coulter. It had been inscribed, autograph style. "I've been framed, S.J. Coulter."

Harry dropped the frame like it was hot. His mind raced. Rock? What did they mean *rock*? Oh, damn. What if Layla had opened this? It was one thing to come after him. He shot out of his chair and took off for the front of the office at a run.

"Layla! Dani!" He shouted their names though he knew the office was empty. He was almost to the door when he looked through the plate-glass windows and saw a small cluster of people gathered near the drained fountain in the center of the atrium. Among them were Layla and Danielle, Deputy Lori Cabrera and Julianne Shields, the sheriff's department's dispatcher.

"What happened?" he demanded, breathless. "What's going on? Is anyone hurt?" he said, scanning each woman for injury as he skidded to a halt near the group.

Layla swiveled, her eyes wide and frightened. "Someone threw a rock through the window."

Harry rushed over to them. Shaking his head, he gazed down at the shaken young woman. "Are you okay?"

"I'm fine," she said a shade too quickly.

"What window? I didn't see any broken glass."

"It was in the break room," Danielle informed him. "I was up at the county clerk's desk, but Layla was in the office."

Lori Cabrera spoke up. "We think they meant to throw through your office window but miscounted."

Harry blinked at her. This was a perfectly reasonable explanation. At least as reasonable as anything was these days. It would be easy to get it wrong. The municipal building had been built in the 1960s. The floor-to-ceiling windows on the interior were meant to allow light to shine inside, but the exterior windows were built high on the walls and embedded in brick. A person couldn't simply walk by the building and peer inside. Such windows kept things bright enough while keeping the relentless South Georgia heat out. They also provided security for the law enforcement and legal professionals who worked in those offices.

"Where is this rock?" Harry demanded.

Lori held up a large zip bag with a smooth brown river rock about eight inches in diameter inside. "There was a note rubber banded to it," she reported.

"Of course there was," Harry snapped, unable to keep the snarky edge out of his tone. "I bet it said something to the effect of 'Free Coulter!'"

Before Lori could confirm or deny, Layla nodded like a bobblehead doll. Harry swallowed his anger and impatience. He couldn't get worked up. He needed to remain calm so all those around him did so too.

He gave Layla's shoulder an awkward pat. "Were you in the break room when it happened?"

She shook her head. "No, but I was in there like

two minutes before," she said with a shudder. "I was restocking the fridge with water, because I thought you'd be back from Judge Nichols's office soon. I made myself a cup of coffee. I'd just gone back to my desk."

Harry clenched his jaw, but he looked her directly in the eye when he spoke. "I'm glad you aren't injured, and I'm sorry you're scared." He gave her a wan half smile. "You said you wanted to get some experience in a DA's office before you started law school. I know this isn't exactly what you had in mind, but sometimes this is the reality of it, Layla." He straightened and glanced around their group. "Sometimes, stuff like this comes with the territory. We prosecute bad people. Bad people associate with other bad people, and sometimes they think they can intimidate us out of doing our jobs, but they can't."

He snapped his mouth shut and shifted his gaze from one person to the next.

"I realize I am not the lead on this case, but for some reason they are singling me out, and I refuse to back down," he said firmly. "Having stated my intention to make my stand, the last thing I want to do is put any of you in danger." Locking eyes with Layla, he said, "If either of you wish to take a leave of absence or find a way to try to do some of your work remotely, I have no issue with giving you some flexibility."

He then zoomed in on his assistant district attorney. "Same goes for you. But I want you both to know I won't be scared into quitting." He rolled his shoulders back and took a deep breath. "I am scared, but I'm not quitting."

"We've got your back, Harry," Deputy Cabrera said gruffly.

He nodded, then shifted his attention to the two women who worked for him. "There's nothing wrong with being scared. But if this is the career you want, if this is the path you're going to choose to take, you're going to have to find a way to tamp down your fear, as well. I don't mind admitting I'm scared. I don't like having my home and office violated. I don't like having the people around me frightened and intimidated. If I could do my job in a way where I wouldn't have to deal with these sorts of things, I would. Do you understand me?"

The two women nodded, then stepped out of the small knot of people. He glanced at Lori. "Have you got enough of a statement?"

The deputy nodded, and Julianne, the dispatcher, reached over to pat Layla on the shoulder.

"I think we're good here, Harry," Lori said. "Keep watching your step. Let us know anytime anything happens. Anything at all," she ordered.

He nodded and then gestured for the two other women to follow him back into the justice side of the law-and-justice center. As he reached for the door handle to hold it open, he spun around and called out to Lori Cabrera.

"Oh, and, Deputy?"

Lori drew to a stop. "Yes?"

"I'd like to RSVP for Saturday," he called across the atrium, holding up two fingers.

The exterior door opened and Alicia walked through holding a white bakery bag. "Hey," she said, dividing the greeting with a glance between himself and Lori. "What's Saturday? Am I missing something?"

Lori suddenly tucked the evidence bag behind her leg, then shot a pointed look at Harry. "Nothing Harry can't fill you in on. See you guys on Saturday, and hopefully not before."

The moment the door to the sheriff's department whooshed closed behind Lori, Alicia looked at him questioningly. "Well, I guess she told you. What's Saturday?" she asked again.

He forced a smile but knew it wasn't quite enough. "We've been invited to our first Christmas party."

Alicia's eyes narrowed as she approached him. "A Christmas party? Isn't it still a bit early for those?"

Harry shrugged. "It's after Thanksgiving, so I think any Saturday is fair game," he said, trying to inject a note of lightness into his tone. But Alicia wasn't fooled.

"What's going on?"

"The usual," he said dismissively. "I got a rock thrown through the break-room window this morning and a framed photograph of Samuel Coulter sent to me by someone using my sister's return address."

Alicia, in all her wisdom, zeroed in on exactly

what was bothering him most. "Your sister's address?"

He tipped his head in the affirmative. "Exactly. But postmarked in Atlanta."

"So whoever this is either actually knows you and your family or has enough knowledge of you to get access to personal information."

Sighing, he released the door and let it swing shut, leaving them alone in the echoing atrium. "It isn't too hard to get personal information. You don't have to be much of a computer hacker to dig up people's addresses these days."

Alicia pondered for a moment. "No, probably not. But unless you've got a bunch of programmers who decided they were born to be wild, it might discount your biker gang."

He sent her an arch look. "Aren't you being presumptive? For all you know, each one of those guys has a PhD."

Alicia nodded in concession. "You're right. I was typecasting. In my defense, I haven't had any caffeine and I'm not sure my brain knows how to function without it. Speaking of caffeine, I think I blew our cover."

"How so?"

"I didn't know you don't drink coffee. Mrs. Brewster had to tell me."

"Ah, yeah, well, it's kind of new. I broke the habit a year or so ago."

She pulled a face. "Sorry. She may be suspicious

now. If we were in a real relationship, I'd know you were a freak of nature."

"You can tell her I've been hiding my dirty secret from you. Camille loves to be in the know."

She frowned as she looked down at her hand and then back up at him, lifting it as if she'd completely forgotten she was holding a white paper bag. "I brought you something."

Sheer surprise made his heart skip a beat. "You did?"

She nodded solemnly. "I bought all three because I didn't know which one you would prefer, but now I'm thinking you probably need all of them."

He took the bag from her and unrolled the top. Peering inside, he saw three doughnuts. One glazed, one cinnamon twist and one cream-filled. This time, there was no holding back his smile. "I think you've mistaken me for a police officer."

"Now who's typecasting?"

Harry chuckled, then gestured toward the door. As he pulled it open for her, he said, "You forget, I've watched Ben Kinsella demolish a box of doughnuts."

She looked back at him over her shoulder as she passed him and led the way toward his office. "Good. Then you won't mind if I eat the cream-filled."

Harry sobered instantly. "Have you not had any breakfast yet?" He took two quick steps to fall in beside her. "I told you to help yourself to anything you wanted."

She shot him a sidelong glance. "You operate

under the assumption I know how to cook. Now we're back to the typecast thing again."

"You could be typecast yourself by claiming you are a woman so focused on her career, she never bothered to learn how to cook."

She smirked as she waltzed into his office and plopped into one of the guest chairs. "Another case of a cliché coming true."

Harry dropped the doughnut bag on his desk, then held up a finger. "Hang tight—I'll be right back."

When he stepped back out of his office, Layla was hanging up the phone. "Maintenance is going to be right up to put some plywood over the window," she reported.

Harry nodded. "Thank you for calling them. Are you sure you're okay?"

"I'm fine. I was freaked, you know?" she said, tucking her hair behind her ear.

Harry let out a bitter laugh. "Yeah, I know."

"If you don't mind, I think I will head home for the day," she said cautiously. "I only need—"

He held up a hand. "No need to explain. Go ahead and take the day. Call or text me to let me know how you're doing, okay?"

She nodded, then reached into the bottom drawer of her desk for her purse. "I will."

Harry stood back for a moment watching as the young woman gathered her belongings. She left with a self-conscious wave. When she was gone, he walked toward the break room. On his way, he poked his head into Danielle's office. "Are you sticking around today, or do you want to head out too?"

Danielle released an indelicate snort. "Not scared of rocks, Harry."

"Neither am I, per se," he said pointedly. "But there have been other threats—one implying it may be more than a rock next time. If you wanted to avoid the office until we figure this out, no one would blame you."

She inclined her head. "Noted, boss. For now, I think I'm going to finish this motion and keep moving ahead." She made a swimming gesture with her hand. "You know I'm a shark."

He smiled. "I know you are."

He crossed into the break room to grab a few paper napkins and a plate. The cool December breeze poured in through the hole in the window. Harry scowled but refused to give it more than a moment's notice. Hustling back to his office, he entered to find Alicia standing in front of his desk staring down at the pile of mail he had opened in the moments before discovering this last bout of vandalism.

"Snooping?" he asked as he strode into the room.

"Admiring the fan art," she replied, nodding to the framed photo of Samuel Coulter. "We need to bag those as evidence."

"I know."

He made a slow circle, then spotted the plastic grocery bag from the Piggly Wiggly in his trash can. "This will do for now. I'll call Lori and have her come get it." Using the letter opener, he finagled the note, envelope and framed photo into the bag, then dropped it on his credenza.

"I wonder if this is his handwriting," Alicia mused as she dug into the bakery bag.

Harry shrugged and handed over the plate and a paper napkin. "I couldn't tell you, but I'm sure someone will be able to."

"I had a nice talk with Marlee Masters this morning. She said she and Lori Cabrera were going to help me get in good with some of the ladies around town," she said with a saucy smile. "Apparently, folks around here don't cotton to strangers," she said, exaggerating her drawl.

He laughed, then extracted the cinnamon twist from the bag, wrapping it in a napkin as he sat down in his desk chair. "I'd like to say it isn't true, but I don't wanna be a liar." He took a giant bite of the doughnut, then, using his free hand, extracted the printed invitation to Simon's Christmas party from the pile. "I believe they concocted this plan without getting you to sign on first," he said, waving the heavy card stock in her direction.

Alicia looked up, the cream-filled doughnut held aloft between her thumb and middle finger. "Oh?"

"We've been invited to a Christmas party, remember?" His smile grew sly as he rocked back in his chair, peeling back the napkin and preparing to take another bite of his doughnut. "I believe Ms. Masters and Deputy Cabrera have arranged your debutante party."

Chapter Eleven

"Come in, come in!" Simon Wingate said, standing back to wave Harry and Alicia across his threshold. Alicia blinked at the man's effusive greeting. His whole demeanor seemed lighter and brighter since Coulter, his former client, had been arraigned and held without bail. Taken aback, but not willing to show it, Alicia plastered a smile on her face as their host gave Harry's hand a hearty shake. She stepped into the warmth of the foyer and nearly jumped out of her skin when Simon whipped a bunch of broccoli from behind his back and held it over her head.

"What do you know? Mistletoe, right here in the entry. Almost doesn't seem fair," he said, leaning in and tapping his cheek to indicate she should kiss him.

Harry snorted, pulling Simon back a couple of steps to give her some room. "Watch it. She can take you down in more ways than you can count."

To his credit, Simon appeared mildly chastened. Offering Alicia a weak smile, he said, "Sorry. Not well done of me. I was trying to get under Harry's skin."

"Well, it worked," Harry growled. "Has to be the lamest excuse for mistletoe I've ever seen," he added derisively. "I can't believe Lori's letting you get away with that."

"Lori's not letting him get away with anything," the woman in question said, entering the foyer. She snatched the broccoli from Simon's hand and threw it directly at the man's forehead. "For someone so smart, you sure do like to act a fool sometimes."

Lori turned to Alicia and offered an apologetic smile. "I'm so sorry. Somebody gets overexcited when he hosts social gatherings and forgets about important things like consent and personal space. I'm sending him to obedience school next week."

"I'm not a dog," Simon retorted, tossing the broccoli back to Lori.

She snagged it midair. "Stop acting like one." She rolled her eyes at her boyfriend's antics. "You're going to scare her off. She's not used to obnoxious men like you."

Simon let out a snort and closed the front door. "I don't think I could scare this woman if I tried. And how do you know what kind of men she's accustomed to being around? I'm willing to bet some of those federal agents are downright obnoxious." He turned to Alicia. "Am I wrong?"

She gave a chuckle. "I can absolutely say you are not wrong." She thrust the bottle of wine they'd brought with them into Simon's hand. "He wasn't nearly this rambunctious the last time I saw him."

Lori rolled her eyes. "He was regretting his god-awful taste in clientele," she said, glaring at Simon while making the pronouncement. "Weren't you?"

"I rue the day," Simon responded, his expression sober. "Can we all forget my past indiscretions and move on knowing I am the charming and lovable guy you see standing in front of you?"

Alicia shrugged. "If she can forgive you, I think any of us could."

Which was true. When Alicia first came to Pine Bluff, Lori and Simon had an intense sort of vibe between them. It was obvious to anyone with eyes there was an attraction, but Lori was hell-bent on bringing Simon's most important client down. It took some time and careful maneuvering for Simon to wriggle out of his attorney-client relationship. Alicia was glad to see the enmity she'd witnessed between the deputy and the defense attorney morph into something happier. By the time she'd left town, there was no doubt Lori and Simon would end up together, and now here they were.

Simon smiled, and Alicia nearly had to take a step back. He was almost as blindingly handsome as Marlee Masters was golden. No one could blame Lori Cabrera for falling hard for a man she didn't entirely trust. She'd fought it. In the end, Alicia gave the younger woman credit for going with her gut. Wingate was one of those guys who could talk the bark off a tree. Unlike Harry, whose good looks and approach to life were shades more understated. But not any less appealing. At least, not to her.

"Where do you want us to throw our jackets?" Harry asked, and Alicia exhaled some of the tension she hadn't realized she was holding.

His pragmatism was a balm to her. His calm in the face of Simon's exuberance made her grateful to have him by her side. For a woman who prided herself on keeping an even keel, she was beginning to feel a bit scattershot in the face of Harry's unshakable cool. Through everything happening to him in the past few weeks, she'd only seen him lose his temper in brief flare-ups, though she knew the man had to be raging inside.

As was she. Bronson had sent her a text. Apparently, he was regretting sending his favorite minion away and insisted she be back in the Atlanta office Monday morning. When she explained what was happening to Harry, he told her the protection of a local district attorney was outside the scope of her job, and unless she had something solid leading to further drug-trafficking arrests, he would see her in his office or she'd find herself on disciplinary leave.

"You may want to hang on to them," Lori said, waving them toward the back of the house. "Everyone is in the kitchen or on the patio. We have a fire going," she explained. "I will show you where the refreshments are."

Harry slipped out of his leather jacket. Ever the

gentleman, he held the collar of her coat so she could shed it more easily. Lori took their jackets and led them to the back of the house.

In the kitchen, she offered Harry his coat again and he blinked at it in confusion. She gestured to the sliding doors to the patio. "Most of the men are out there. They have made fire. They must stand by fire and drink beer as men do," she said, grunting each word in a bad caveman impression.

Harry rolled his eyes. "Gee, thanks. I love being classified by my gender as a Neanderthal. For the record, I cook, and I cook well."

Lori laughed. And Alicia watched as her hostess casually tossed her coat onto a mound piled on a bench near the back door. "You can complain to us about gender inequalities in about two or three hundred years. In the meantime, scram. I want to talk to Alicia and I don't want you around," Lori said, tipping her chin up and defying him to contradict her.

"You're a lot bossier here than you are at work."

"I'm not the boss of you at work," Lori shot back without missing a beat.

Harry checked with Alicia, silently making sure she was okay with the plan. She nodded vigorously. This was exactly how she wanted the evening to go. Alicia had taken Marlee's words at the bakery to heart.

Divide and conquer. She would let Marlee and Lori pave the way for her with the women of Pine

Bluff. There was no better way to know the pulse of a place than to get in with the locals.

"Run along. Don't set yourself on fire," she said dismissively. "We've had enough excitement for one week."

"I concur," Harry said dryly. He lifted a hand in farewell and made his way toward the patio.

The second the sliding door was pulled shut, Lori took Alicia by the elbow and escorted her to the hall. "You have had a heck of a week. Are you sure you're up for a party tonight?"

"I am most definitely up for a party tonight," Alicia stated, meeting the other woman's gaze directly. "And I'm counting on you to tell me who I need to get to know."

Lori's eyes narrowed, but her lips curved up and she gave an appreciative nod. "Marlee will be here soon, and between the two of us, we're going to introduce you to everybody who's anybody in Pine Bluff."

"And will those everybodies who know anybody have any clue as to who might be doing some of the things happening to Harry?"

"If they don't know them directly, they will have knowledge about them," Lori declared. "We haven't told too many people what you do for a living," she said quietly.

Alicia quirked an eyebrow. "Cool. Thank you."

"It's a good idea," Lori said. "First of all, you're a Fed, and people around here are still wary of the

DEA. The methamphetamine busts a couple years ago threw the town into a tailspin. There have been ongoing repercussions for a lot of families. They are also wary around me and Ben because we're 'the law,'" she said, using air quotes. "Country folks get a bit touchy about people nosing in their business. Even people they know." She sighed. "They're going to be even more on their guard if they know you're with the DEA. So for our purposes tonight, I'm going to be introducing you as Harry's girlfriend."

Alicia startled, taken aback at hearing the label spoken out loud.

"If they ask how you met, be vague. Tell them you consulted on a case or something—don't get too specific," Lori said in a low voice. "They'll want to pry, but they want to pry more about you personally and professionally."

Alicia swallowed hard, and a small knot of panic tightened her stomach. "Personally? Like what kind of personal stuff?"

Lori dismissed Alicia's worries with a wave. "Like the romantic personal stuff. And it's none of their business. But they want the story, so make up a good one. Go with the old 'Our eyes met across a conference table and I couldn't resist him.'" She circled a hand to indicate this was enough to get the ball rolling. "The next thing you knew, the two of you were throwing down."

The notion was so ludicrous, a laugh burbled out of Alicia. "Throwing down."

Lori grinned. "I know it's silly, but people around here like a juicy story, so don't be shy about embellishing. The more they think they know about you, the more they'll be apt to tell you about themselves. People in small towns are like eggs. They have a tough shell, but once you crack the outer coating, it's all going to come spilling out."

TWO HOURS LATER, Alicia could say without a doubt Lori wasn't lying.

She'd been introduced to everyone from Simon's grandfather Wendell—a dapper older man whose honey-eyed drawl made Alicia think of porch rockers, seersucker suits and mint juleps—to a woman named Susie Troutman, who obviously prided herself on being the town's font of information. Alicia didn't know exactly how it happened, but she found herself squished into a love seat in the living room with a hairdresser named Shelly on one side, Susie the talker on the other and a shrewd woman named Trudy parked in a nearby armchair, watching Alicia like a hawk.

Harry had popped into the room, she assumed to check on her, and all the women cooed. It turned out, Harry was a natural at this whole "act like we're together" thing. He strolled in with a beer in one hand and a bottle of water for her. Their audience watched appreciatively as he handed over the water and asked if she needed anything from the overburdened buffet set up on the dining-room table. He oh-so-casually pressed a kiss to her forehead before wandering away again. When he was out of earshot, they pounced, demanding to know how they had met.

She and Lori exchanged an amused smirk before she cautiously started to spin a tale. "Well, I knew Ben in Atlanta." She paused, not wanting to say they worked together because someone might be able to add one and one and come up with the DEA. "We kinda ran in the same circles," she added with a wave of her hand. "Anyway, I came down here to visit a few months ago."

When they all nodded, she faced Marlee. With a slight incline of her head, Marlee signaled her to say whatever needed to be said. "The truth is, I was single, and I was hoping to find Ben was too when I came down here," she confessed, leaning closer to Susie. She fixed Marlee with a playful glare. "Unfortunately, I was too late."

"You snooze, you lose," Marlee called back.

"I guess so. Anyway, I had been laid off at my job, and Marlee and I got to talking, and the next thing I knew, she offered me a position with Timber Masters. I'm telling you, it was a godsend," she said, shifting her attention to hairdresser Shelly.

Almost on cue, the other woman pressed her hand to her chest and opened her eyes wide. "Nothing short of divine providence," she said with a nod, prompting the others to agree.

Alicia did her best not to smile when she saw a few other heads bob in agreement. "She's a saint. I met Harry through Ben and Marlee." She ended with a shrug, but a sharp elbow from Lori told her the story wasn't going to cut it in terms of being juicy enough. Thankfully, Marlee picked up the baton.

"She came down here to try to steal my man," she said with a broad smile. "I had to explain to her how those of us who grew up here in Masters County protect what's ours, but I was taught to be generous with what I have, and I try to be. With everything except my man," she added with a playful glare.

There was a general murmur of laughter and good-natured agreement. Alicia ducked her head, and her cheeks warmed. She hoped the blush was visible.

"Honestly, I wasn't trying to steal anybody's guy. Last I'd known, he was fair game."

"I was afraid she'd start making eyes at Simon," Lori interjected.

Alicia's eyebrows rose right along with everybody else's. "I did not."

"Only because I was onto you." Lori sniffed and rolled her shoulders back, assuming the confident posture of a woman who knew she had her man wrapped up tight. "But I can't blame you. The man is hot."

There was another general murmur of agreement as a couple of other women drifted over from other conversations, deepening the circle around the love seat.

"Y'all are making me sound desperate and man-hungry," Alicia argued. She turned to Shelly the hairdresser. "Do I give off some kind of man-hungry vibe?"

The other woman pursed her lips as if giving the question serious consideration. "No. I think if you were man-hungry, you'd have had some highlights done or something."

Alicia barked a laugh. "Exactly."

As if summoned, Simon Wingate appeared in the doorway to the living room. "Did I hear somebody in here is man-hungry?"

There was a general chorus of nos and orders to go away. Chuckling, he raised his hands in surrender and backed out of his own living room.

"You already have more woman than you can handle, mister," Lori called after him.

Simon's response floated back to them. "Don't I know it."

"I didn't come here to steal anyone's man. You know how it is when your whole life is turned upside down," she said, turning to the skeptical woman in the chair nearby. "I wanted a fresh start."

"But you didn't stick around long," Marlee said with a chuckle. "I know it's hard to find good people these days, but usually people stay in my employment for longer than three weeks before they get a better offer and move on."

Alicia rolled with it. "Aw, you know I'm sorry about having to leave so quickly. It was too good to pass up," she said with a helpless shrug. Turning back to Susie, she explained, "I was recruited by a headhunter for a big firm back in Atlanta. They were offering the sun and the moon, and I was already at the point where I was going to have to sublet my condo to make the mortgage payment. It didn't make sense to stay here."

"But what about Harry?" the woman named Trudy asked, finally leaning in a bit. "Wouldn't he have been reason enough to stay?"

Alicia wanted to say something pithy about setting the women's movement back another fifty years but bit her cheek. She wasn't there to sermonize; she was supposed to be making friends.

She tried for a sort of downcast, dejected pose, but wasn't sure she quite got it right. So she did the next best thing. She threw Harrison Hayes under the bus.

"He didn't ask me to."

The statement earned her another chorus of awws and more than a few disgruntled mutters about men in general. Pleased, she decided she could pull off magnanimous as well as Marlee Masters could.

"To be fair, we had barely started seeing each other," she said in a rush, hoping they would appreciate how quickly she rose to defend poor Harry's honor. "We both did the whole no harm, no foul, let's keep in touch, play-it-casual thing," she said, offering a self-deprecating smile.

"And how long did you last?" Lori prodded.

Alicia ducked her head again. When she peeked at Susie Troutman from under her eyelashes, she saw she had the woman eating out of her palm. "Three days," she replied quietly. "He lasted three days."

All the women in the room sighed with pleasure, and *voila!* The egg was cracked.

Alicia spent the next hour and a half sitting on the love seat, soaking up every tidbit of information she could like a sponge.

By the time Harry appeared in the doorway holding her coat, her head was spinning and her bladder near to bursting. Anxious to talk over her newly gleaned information with Harry, she wriggled her way off the love seat, making all the right noises about how she hated to leave her new friends, but she couldn't keep her man waiting.

When she reached him, she took her coat from his arm and leaned in close. "I need the powder room before we try to walk home from here."

He nodded to a door at the end of the hallway. "There's one there, but if it's occupied, I'm sure Simon wouldn't mind you heading down to the bedroom to use the master."

Alicia chuckled at his use of the term. "Hang tight. I'll be right back."

Before she could step away, he plucked her coat out of her hand once more. "I'll be right here."

Five minutes later, they'd said their goodbyes and thanked Lori and Simon for a nice evening. Alicia found herself laughing as they made their way down the shallow porch steps. "That was interesting."

He smiled down at her. "Good interesting?"

"Mostly, I'd say," she assured him.

Their breaths floated away in clouds of vapor. Alicia tucked her hands into her jacket pockets and scanned the street as they turned onto the sidewalk. Most every house boasted some kind of Christmas decor, some more understated than others. "People around here seriously start Christmas the minute Thanksgiving is over, don't they?"

Harry paused to take in the scene as if noticing for the first time. "What? Oh, well, it's no different from anywhere else. Retail-driven holiday spirit. Seems like we skip right over Thanksgiving anymore."

"True." She walked beside him, noticing how nicely the length of their strides matched. "I heard a couple of interesting things tonight."

He slid her a sidelong glance. "Oh?"

She nodded. "Do you know someone named Rinker?"

Harry made a sound of assent. "Yeah. Chet Rinker owns the pharmacy. Why?"

"Hmm." She filed the information away to be examined more closely later. "I guess he's developed an interest in motorcycles. Been running with a bunch of hoodlums, according to Susie Troutman." He stopped dead in his tracks. When she turned back, she found him scowling fiercely. "What?"

"Chet Rinker?" he demanded.

She let one shoulder rise and fall. "She called him *That Rinker boy.*"

Some of the confusion clouding his face cleared. "She must have meant Matt Rinker, Chet's son."

"Okay."

Alicia raised an eyebrow. She couldn't care less whether the person in question was father or son. She was focused solely on the notion of someone local keeping company with people the townsfolk obviously disapproved of. Add in the pharmacy angle, the rise of oxy addicts and heroin usage in the area, and suddenly her curiosity was more than piqued.

Harry started walking again, and she had to jog two steps to catch up when he passed her, his gaze fixed somewhere beyond the end of the block.

"Do you know him?" she asked, falling back into step beside him.

"He was younger than me in school, so not well."

Alicia didn't need to prod more to know whether they were good friends or not; Harry was affronted by the idea of this Matt Rinker coming after him. More so than he had been about the Smithson guy who had been in the same year.

Fascinated by what appeared to be another wrinkle in the small-town dynamic, she pushed. "But you're upset it might be him."

"Well, of course I am," he retorted. He slowed when they approached the corner.

"Why? You said you didn't know him well," she prodded. "Why is it worse for this guy to be in on it than the Smithson guy?"

"Because it is," Harry said, his tone brusque.

They stepped off the curb and were about three strides across the street when the squeal of tires alerted them to the approach of a vehicle. Alicia's head swiveled in time to see a dark sedan with no headlights bearing down on them, the acrid scent of burnt rubber blooming in the crisp night air.

"Harry!" she barked, catching his arm and propelling him forward.

They were aligned with the center of the hood, and Alicia knew they stood a better chance with momentum on their side. He twisted his arm around until it encircled her waist and all but shoved her up onto the opposite curb. Together, they dived into a neatly trimmed hedge strung with white Christmas lights.

Chapter Twelve

Harry turned his head in time to see the car run up on the curb they'd hopped a split second ago, but before he could right himself enough to get a good look at the vehicle, the driver had hooked a sharp left onto the next street and floored it.

"Sedan, older model, no plates," Alicia panted. She wriggled out of Harry's tight hold and rolled off his chest. Grasping a handful of shrubbery, she leveraged herself out of the hedge, then turned to offer him a hand.

"How'd you get all that?" Harry gained his feet, then bent forward, bracing his hands on wobbly knees.

"I saw there was no front tag when it was coming at us. Caught sight of the back before he turned."

"I can't believe you had the presence of mind to do either," he grumbled. "All I could think about was getting out of the way."

She slid down to sit cross-legged on the grass. The corner of her mouth was twisted into a frustrated smirk. "Now, if I'd have been able to catch a tag and memorize it, that would've been impressive."

"Oh, well, yeah. You're right. Way to put forth mediocre effort, Agent Simmons," he said, dropping into a sitting position next to her.

"I'll try to do better next time." With a groan, Alicia rolled onto her hip and rummaged in her pocket.

"Are you okay?" he demanded, panic rising inside him. Of course she wasn't okay. She was pregnant and they were diving into bushes to keep from being run over by cars. "Are you hurt?"

She extracted her cell phone from her jacket pocket. "Oh, thank God I didn't break another one."

"Excuse me?"

She held her phone up and waved it at him. "I didn't break the screen. I'm not exactly easy on phones. I didn't want to have to replace another screen."

He stared at her openmouthed, trying to reconcile his concern for her well-being and the health of their unborn child with her relief at finding her mobile phone intact. "You're worried about your phone?"

Her head popped up. He hadn't been able to check the disapproval in his tone, and Alicia found she had to tamp down her impatience his judgement stirred. "I find cellular devices handy when one has narrowly avoided being mowed down. I need to call Ben and report this."

Harry didn't think; he simply reacted. Reaching

out, he grasped her wrist and kept her from completing the call. "Don't."

She gaped at him, surprised. "Don't? This needs to go on the record."

He reached over and gently removed her phone from her hand and placed it on her leg. He sandwiched her cool fingers between his hands and expelled a long plume of breath. "It doesn't need to be called in right now. We have no make or model, no license plate. I'm not even sure what color it was." He shrugged and chafed her hand to warm it. "Ben's at the party. He's out with his girlfriend having a nice Saturday night. This can keep until tomorrow."

Alicia held his gaze for a beat before nodding. When he didn't let go of her, she dropped her eyes to their joined hands.

"People were asking how we, uh, got together..." She trailed off. "I had to tell them some story about how we got together in exchange for them telling me their stories."

He gave her a half-hearted smile. "The currency of small towns."

She met his eyes again. "The funny thing was, other than Marlee and Lori insinuating I came here with an eye toward stealing their men, I didn't have much to say. It was...there wasn't anybody here who interests me as much as you do," she said with a small lift of her shoulders.

"I'm going to take your interest as a compliment," he warned.

"It was meant as one." Alicia offered him a tremulous smile. "I thought you were interesting, but now I find you downright fascinating."

He let go of her hand. "Fascinating? Hardly."

"But you are. You've got this kind of center of calm and cool I don't often see in people who aren't cops."

He ducked his head, pleased and embarrassed. Anxious to escape her scrutiny, Harry planted a hand on the cool damp grass and pressed up. Once he'd regained his feet, he offered her both of his hands and she placed her fingers in his. "I'm adding *cool* to the pile of compliments."

She shot up and bumped right into his chest. Again. Harry felt a sizzle of excitement. And familiarity. A flashback to the night they'd spent together. He tamped it down. His life was complicated enough right now, and things between him and Alicia were only going to get more complicated as her pregnancy advanced.

"Harry," she prompted, drawing his attention up from where their bodies pressed together to where her eyes bored into his.

He had a flashback to the night they'd been together. The joy and uninhibited pleasure they'd taken in one another. Now they were running on adrenaline and fear, and Harry decided if he were to kiss this woman again, he didn't want it to be because they survived some ordeal together. He wanted to revel in genuine jubilation with her again. He lifted his hands to hers, wrapped them firmly around her fingers and gave them a gentle squeeze before removing them from his chest.

"Come on. Let's go home."

HOME. HE'D SAID the word so casually. Thoughtlessly, probably, but Alicia couldn't stop thinking about it. Thinking about him. Or about the people who were trying to make him feel uncomfortable in the town he considered his home. Alicia stared up at the ceiling long into the night. Harry's guest room was comfortable, though the decor was somewhat on the masculine, minimalist side, but lived-in. Truth be told, she liked it this way. Her own condo in Atlanta was more like a room at one of those extended-stay hotels. Probably one of the reasons why she didn't consider it home.

Home.

She tossed and turned, trying to parse out why it sounded so right when Harry said *Let's go home.* Given her background, she didn't need an advanced degree to make sense of it. He was home. Pine Bluff was his home; this house was his home. One of the women at the party had told her it had once been his parents' house, so it may even have been the home he grew up in.

Alicia tried to imagine living in any of the myriad houses her parents had either purchased or rented depending on how long her father's post was expected to last. She wondered if it was weird for him, living as an adult in the house where he'd been a boy. Had this been his room at one time? She'd seen another bedroom converted into a home office. Had it been strange for him to move into the larger master bedroom at the end of the hall? Maybe not. The redhead who told her the house once belonged to his parents also said Harry had put a lot of work into making the place his own.

Why hadn't she thought about inspecting his place in the hours he was gone? Why had she stuck so close to the public rooms of the house and not poked her nose in at least a couple of his drawers? Frankly, it was unlike her. She was a cop. Sure, they put the title Special Agent in front of her name, but when it came down to it, she was no different from any other member of the law enforcement community. Her lack of curiosity in this case would have been considered appalling by some of her colleagues.

But she didn't want to cross any lines with Harry.

He was obviously a man who liked structure and boundaries. She was a guest in his home and had no desire to pry into the private life of her host. Okay, she had the desire, but she had more willpower. She knew enough about him as it was. Probably more than he'd want her to know if she hadn't borne witness to the attacks on him.

Restless, she flung back the covers, swung her legs from the bed and padded to the dresser where she'd left her laptop. She might not be willing to go through his bathroom cabinet, but she wasn't at all above poking in some dark corners to determine exactly how real these threats were. Up until this point, the bumbling attempts to intimidate him could be considered scare tactics, some more extreme than others, but tonight…

Tonight, someone meant to cause them bodily harm.

Some ancient maternal instinct had her covering her still-flat abdomen with her hand. As if she could somehow reassure herself the child she was carrying was nevertheless safe and secure.

Ridiculous, she thought, snatching the laptop from the dresser and hurrying back to the warmth of her bed. With the duvet pulled up over her bare legs, she flipped open the top and booted the computer.

It opened to her email application automatically, but Alicia shut it down after ingesting the gist of Bronson's email. He'd put his order in writing. An email from his agency address made his order more official than the text massage. He expected to see her Monday morning, or else.

The ultimatum meant she had less than twenty-four hours to make a decision that would likely affect the rest of her career.

Instead, with a few quick keystrokes, she logged in to a message board. It appeared to be a chat room like any other, but this was a site most people would never stumble across on their own. One of the tech guys at work clued her in to it when she asked about how to search out hate groups. She only had to try two different variations of search terms before she found some hits. The name Samuel Coulter spawned more than one thread. Only two had regular interchanges, so she zeroed in on them.

Drawing a deep breath, she clicked on the one titled "Samuel Coulter was framed" and scrolled back through the messages until she found the post at the head of the thread. Her stomach churned while she absorbed conspiracy theory after conspiracy theory. Her gorge rose when she read each justification for Coulter's acquittal.

Most of these posters had absolutely no idea who or what they were dealing with. They simply thought a man who dealt in exotic snakes had been framed by the federal government as a drug trafficker to stop them from pursuing their hobby.

They were wrong.

The evidence she'd uncovered before coming to Pine Bluff showed Coulter had a long history of involvement with some of South Florida's most infamous traffickers. He had ongoing connections with various gangs in both the Miami and Jacksonville areas. It had been absolutely no surprise to her to discover he was connected with the product moving through Atlanta. Some of the convoluted ideas people posted were plain creepy.

Gnawing her bottom lip, she reached over and switched on the bedside lamp. As Simon Wingate pointed out, she wasn't a woman who scared easily, but she was also human. If she was going to trawl through the dregs of internet society, she could do so with the light on.

She was a half hour in before she found her first direct hit. The person who posted actually typed the name Ivan Jones.

A chill ran down her spine when she scanned the subthreads connected to the entry. She was so absorbed in her research, she barely registered the soft knock on her door. Lowering the top of her laptop, she stared at the door in confusion before whispering a tentative "Come in?" She didn't want to speak too loudly in case she'd only imagined the knock.

The door opened and Harry poked his head in. "Can't sleep?"

Alicia closed the lid on the laptop, not wanting him to know exactly what she was piecing together until it was fully formed in her head. "Restless night."

He opened the door farther, propped his forearm on the jamb and ran his other hand through his already rumpled hair. Alicia took in the view. She was only human, after all. He wore a washed-thin T-shirt and flannel pajama pants. The angle of the arm braced against the door only highlighted the contour of his biceps. The last time she'd seen his hair in such disarray, it had been her fingers doing the mussing.

"Do you think you can eat something?" he asked.

Startled by the offer of food rather than warm milk, cocoa or whatever else people thought they should drink in the middle of the night, she let out a laugh.

It took only a second for the thought to find a foothold, and her stomach growled its affirmative response. "Actually, I think I can."

"Come to the kitchen. I'll make us some oatmeal."

He was gone before she could question his choice of late-night snack. She swung her legs over the edge of the bed and yanked on the yoga pants she'd discarded before climbing between the sheets. She stuffed her bare toes into a pair of fluffy slippers she'd bought on a whim the previous winter. When she scuffed into the kitchen, Harry's gaze trailed to her feet and his eyebrows jumped.

"Never pegged you for the leopard-print type," he commented. "Those are totally something my sister would pick out."

"Every woman is a leopard-print type, under the right circumstances." she asserted with more confidence than she felt. Frankly, she was embarrassed to be caught in the slippers. For some reason, she was afraid he'd find them frivolous, perhaps think less of her as a cop because her choices in footwear weren't always tactical. "But these were an impulse buy. They were on sale, so I grabbed them off the rack."

Lie. She'd seen them online and ordered them specifically because she wanted something pretty.

There were times when being a woman in a male-dominated world wore on her. Times when she wanted to let down her guard and indulge in something simply because it was pretty or fun. These were the sorts of things she had to keep to herself. She indulged by purchasing things no one else would ever see. Of course, she hadn't been living in someone else's house at the time.

Anxious to change the subject, she wrinkled her nose. "Are you actually offering me oatmeal?"

He shrugged. "I can't offer you a brandy or coffee, not that the latter would do anything to make you sleepy." He stretched to reach up onto the top shelf and pull down the familiar round container of oats. "I always found the notion of warm milk kind of gross. Like you're drinking it straight out of the cow, you know?" When she nodded, he gestured to the container. "My mom used to make me oatmeal when I couldn't sleep. It's surprisingly effective. It's warm, filling and, with a splash of milk and a sprinkle of brown sugar, pretty comforting."

Alicia stepped over to the counter. "Okay, you've convinced me."

He smiled. "Good. If you would—"

Alicia didn't know what he was going to ask her to do. It probably wasn't kiss him. But kiss him she did. When he turned toward her, his smile brightening his too serious features, and his hair sticking up in all directions, there wasn't much else she could do.

If it came right down to it, she could blame it on the adrenaline. Somebody had tried to kill them tonight. Somebody had been taking shots at him.

There, in his semidark kitchen, Alicia hadn't been able to stand the thought of going another minute without kissing him again.

In case.

His lips were warm and soft, parted in surprise. It took only a heartbeat, but he quickly caught on. Their lips clung when she pulled back. She hated to end the kiss, but she wanted to be clear whether the movement of his mouth against hers had been one of acquiescence or objection. She needed to get a tighter rein on herself until she knew whether he even wanted to be kissed.

"Sorry," she whispered. "Kinda like the slippers—poor impulse control."

Lips still parted, he gave his head a slight shake. "You have to try another excuse because I'm never going to buy impulse control."

"We almost died tonight."

"I'm not sure I'm going to go with near death either," he said. "People been taking shots at us for a while now. You haven't felt compelled to kiss me after any of them."

"How do you know?" she shot back. "Maybe I did, and I held back."

"Completely blowing your story about the poor impulse control," he said, bringing the argument full circle. "Admit you wanted to kiss me."

They stood toe to toe, their eyes locked on one another. "I wanted to kiss you."

"I'm glad. I've been wanting to kiss you since you first showed up on my doorstep."

"Liar," she said with a sly smile. "You never would've called me if I hadn't shown up on your doorstep."

"Never is a pretty firm stance to take," he said. "If I'd had any indication you would've been receptive to a call, I would have, but all markers pointed to you wanting to make a clean escape."

A laugh bubbled out of her, and she patted her stomach. "So much for my plan."

He reached down and covered her hand with his. "I'm glad it didn't work out."

His fingers splayed over hers. She was carrying their child. It seemed absurd to get butterflies in her stomach when she'd already been with this man. Would be connected to this man for the rest of her life. But still, she felt as edgy and excited as she'd been the night he'd driven her home from Simon Wingate's party back in the fall.

But she had to be clear. If they were going to blur the line, she had to know they were on the same page.

"So, you want to kiss me?"

"Yes," he answered simply.

She smiled, loving how he instinctively knew he needed to take the most direct routes with her. "Okay, so kissing is on the table," she said, speaking slowly.

When she didn't go on, he quirked an eyebrow. "On the table? Doesn't sound sanitary."

She laughed again and reached up to smooth his

hair into place. "I like you, Harry. I've always liked you," she said with a helpless shrug. "If I didn't like you, I never would've slept with you."

"I like you too," he said, his face settling back into its usual sober expression. "And I like kissing you."

She nodded. "Okay. Good. But things are pretty complicated right now, so maybe we should leave it for tonight."

"Makes sense. For the record, I hate making sense right now," he clarified.

She knew in that moment there was no way she was leaving for Atlanta the following morning. Bronson could reprimand her if he wanted, but she was sticking. For now. Maybe for a while. She'd have to see.

Aware she was getting way ahead of herself, needing a diversion, she nudged him with her elbow and nodded to the container of oats in front of him. "Are we going to stand here talking all night, or are you gonna make me some mush?"

Chapter Thirteen

They passed Sunday in the haze of exhaustion and hyperawareness. Alicia hadn't kissed him again, and he hadn't made a move in her direction either. It didn't feel right. Not because he wasn't attracted to her, but because there was too much going on for him to open up another line of worry.

His reasoning was lame, and he knew it.

She was already in his life. Would be for at least the next nineteen years, if not for a lifetime. And though he hadn't completely wrapped his mind around the thought of being a father, he found himself thinking about being with Alicia way too often. Which called up the question of motivation. He didn't want her to be with him because of the baby, and he didn't want to not be with her because of the baby.

Harry heaved a sigh and flipped on the buzzing overhead lights, trudging toward his office. It was only six thirty in the morning, and barely light outside, but after a day of dancing around her in his house, Harry needed an escape. Work seemed the perfect place to go.

He tossed his briefcase on the chair inside his office and made his way to the break room. The broken window had a piece of plywood covering the hole. As far as Harry could see, there had been no additional damage over the weekend. He pulled a bottle of water from the fridge and an orange from the bowl of fruit on the counter. He'd need to make a run to the Piggly Wiggly this week to restock it. He dug his thumbnail into the rind and made his way back to his office.

Yesterday, Alicia had remarked on his eating habits, asking if he was some kind of a monk or if self-deprivation was his particular brand of kink. He frowned at the orange in his hand. He tried to explain he wasn't a foodie. He saw food as fuel, and if he was going to put fuel in his tank, he tried to go for the premium. But he was no health nut. He loved pizza and pasta and a giant plate of tamales as much as the next guy.

She'd laughed at him, and the throaty sound of it made him want to kiss her again. Despite her skill in teasing, she was not a woman who laughed often. He liked the surprise of it. He wasn't anyone's idea of a class cutup either. But he didn't care if he was the butt of the joke or not; he was happy to be the guy who made her laugh. Dropping into his chair, he pulled his trash can out from under the desk and quickly and efficiently peeled the orange. The scent of citrus filled the air while he broke segments from the fruit and bit into its juicy pulp.

Between her morning, noon and night sickness, and his naturally not-voracious appetite, they'd managed to make it through a day with a container of soup and a couple of sandwiches. After she had disappeared into her room the night before, he'd made up for her lack of supper by hoovering an entire bag of tortilla chips.

Now his stomach was growling, demanding more fuel before he could start his day. He tipped the bottle of water to his mouth and chugged three-quarters of it down in long gulps. Being in the office was a relief. The quiet closed around him like a warm blanket. He'd become accustomed to a solitary life, and while Alicia was anything but intrusive, she was definitely distracting.

He rocked back in his chair, methodically working his way through the orange. Allowing his mind to drift. She'd seemed edgy the previous day. Like something was weighing on her. But she didn't offer any reason, and he didn't ask. Truthfully, he was scared she regretted kissing him.

So he stuck to chatting about Simon's party, explaining the backstory behind some of the tales she'd heard. When the conversation turned to the person who'd tried to run them down, Alicia had insisted on lining out a timeline detailing every single threat or bit of damage done to his property or places associated with him. Seeing it all laid out, one sheet of printer paper per incident, nearly blanketed the dining table he rarely used. She'd made a list of all the names she'd noted from the previous evening and pressed him for more. When they finished, she'd nodded decisively and said something about narrowing down some of the searches she was doing in internet chat rooms.

Harry hadn't been surprised to discover she was working the case from her own angles. While he'd never been one for social media or general internet browsing, he appreciated how much data people either willingly or unwittingly gave away.

His own digital footprint was small, but not nonexistent. He had a business profile, and his photo was on the county website. He'd never given it much thought. He was of the opinion the most useful thing the web provided was instant access to sports scores. Any research related to the cases he was working was usually performed by either Danielle or Layla, and the pertinent information sent to him in an email if it needed his immediate attention or added to the client's folder.

Either way, he'd never ventured onto any kind of forum or chat room. The opinions of strangers didn't mean much to him. Truthfully, he found opinions in general worthless. He was a man who dealt in facts. Evidence. Sworn testimony. Anything posted online could be easily fabricated, so he didn't bother with it much. If the rest of the world wanted to get their facts from user-curated sources, he wasn't going to stop them, nor was he going to put his faith in them.

But he knew someone who did.

Drawing his phone from his jacket pocket, he

chewed another segment of orange and scrolled through his contacts. One of his roommates in college had been heavy into computers. Mostly, it seemed he liked the mischief he could make with them, but eventually they gave him a degree, and the degree coupled with his superprocessor brain led him into some high-clearance work in both the public and private sectors.

Randy was the most unlikely computer whiz Harry had ever encountered. Rather than the antisocial hermit holed up in a dark room pecking code into a keyboard, Randy had been a young man determined to live up to his name. He happened to have a skill set that lent itself well to poking around in places where he didn't necessarily belong. Harry suspected this was how the guy ended up on the dean's list every semester even though Harry had hardly ever witnessed Randy hitting the books. A guy with a computer brain probably didn't need to study as hard as mere mortals.

He smirked and tapped the screen to call up his old friend's number, but realized it was still probably too early to call. Switching to a text message, he typed with one thumb.

Hey. Been a long time, but I need to talk to you. Will you call when you get a minute?

Satisfied, Harry set the phone on his desk and turned his attention to finishing his fruit. A few seconds later the screen lit up, and his ringtone echoed through the empty offices. Harry shot forward in his seat and, seeing Randy's name on the screen, quickly swiped to accept the call.

"Hey, man, I know it's early. I didn't mean for you to have to call me right away," Harry said by way of greeting.

"I'm up. There I was, mountain biking in the Andes, and my old friend Harry calls. Bam! Out of the blue," Randy replied jovially. "Isn't modern technology fantastic?"

"You're where?"

Randy chuckled. "I'm in my apartment in DC, but on a virtual trail ride."

His friend did sound winded. "I don't want to interrupt your virtual whatever."

"It's cool. You should try it."

Harry snorted. "You know me. Probably never gonna happen."

The other man laughed, as well. "I do know you, and you're right. You're probably calling me asking me how you can reset your email password."

"I'm not that bad," he demurred. "I've got the basic tasks covered, and I don't need much else."

"You remember Cindy? The girl you dated sophomore year? She's married and has three kids, and she's still too pretty for you," Randy informed him.

"Good old Cindy," Harry replied.

"Aren't you the least bit curious as to what people are doing?" Randy asked.

"Not curious enough to get on whatever platform you're pushing." Harry picked up the water bottle and drained the rest of its contents. "Besides, Cindy sends me a Christmas card every year with one of those newsletters keeping the world up to date on what all the kids are doing."

"Still rocking it old-school." Randy snickered. "It's cool. Of course, I think it's funny you send Christmas cards to your exes, but you won't even get on PicturSpam. Even my grandma had a PicturSpam account."

"I don't send her Christmas cards—she sends Christmas cards to me," Harry corrected.

"Oh, my mistake, Mr. Cool," Randy teased. "What can I do for you bright and early this Monday morning? Are you calling to tell me I'm not getting a Christmas card from you either?"

He sighed. For a guy who could follow the logic of code, Randy remained bafflingly lost when it came to the logic of people. "If I don't send any Christmas cards to anyone, you can assume you are also on my list of non-Christmas-card recipients."

"Cold," Randy replied good-naturedly.

Enjoying the chitchat, but needing to get down to the business of the call, Harry launched himself from his chair and carried his empty water bottle back into the break room. He sandwiched the phone between his ear and a shoulder and held the bottle under the watercooler spigot to refill it. He didn't want another one of Layla's lectures on landfills and the evils of single-use containers.

"Listen, I need to talk to you about how I find one of those forums where people spout off about all sorts of stuff."

This time Randy's laugh was more of a guffaw. "Could you be more specific, dude?"

"You know, like if I had a case and some nutjobs were going to spew a bunch of nonsense on a forum about it, where would they go?"

"Only about a bazillion different places," Randy shot back. "Man, you really have no clue about the internet, do you?"

"I know what I want to know about it," Harry retorted.

"Apparently not, or you wouldn't be calling me asking me how to find, and I quote, 'one of those forums.' Unquote." He added the last word as punctuation.

After carrying his water back to his desk, Harry sat down with a heavy sigh. "Listen, Rand, some-one's been making some threats, okay? They're re-lated to a case I'm involved in. I want to see what's being said in hopes of figuring out who's doing these things."

His friend sobered instantly. "Wait. Doing things or saying things? What kind of things?"

Harry didn't want to give him the nitty-gritty on the more serious stuff, so he dismissed the destruc-tion of his business and personal property with a shrug. "Malicious mischief type stuff. Tire slashing, broken windows, a couple of threatening notes."

"So it's somebody there. Somebody local," Randy answered, suddenly keying in on the people logic.

"The general consensus," Harry said cautiously. "But we think there may be something bigger behind it. Someone fueling some of the fires around here. Prosecutors aren't always the most popular people in town. I want to see what's being said online."

Randy let out a low whistle. "No better place to fan the fires," he commented, all traces of humor gone. "The problem is, most people use screen names or aliases online. You'd have to key in on an IP address and…" He paused as if remembering Harry was still on the call. "You'll never be able to do this. Give me the particulars on the case and who it involves. I'm going to run some searches. I'll get back to you."

"I appreciate you, man," he said gruffly. "The case involves a guy named Samuel Coulter. He's a day trader turned exotic-snake enthusiast."

"Are you kidding me?" Randy asked, chuckling.

"I wish. He was arrested two months ago in a DEA bust involving the trafficking of heroin."

"Whoa," Randy breathed. "No kidding."

This time, Harry smiled. "Nope. Not kidding." He might be naive when it came to the cyberworld, but he had no illusions about what happened right here in real life. "I'm going to give you another name.

He's a local guy, and I'm wondering if we can find some kind of connection between the two of them."

"Fire away," Randy prompted.

"The name is Matthew Rinker. Spelled *R-I-N-K-E-R*," he said, wondering if his friend was taking this information down. He figured if he spelled it out, the information may embed itself in Randy's steel trap of a memory. Still... "Are you writing this down?"

A snicker came through the phone. "No need. Hang on." Randy fumbled with the phone. A second later, Harry heard him say, "New note. Samuel Coulter. Snakes. Trafficking. Heroin. Matthew Rinker. *R-I-N-K-E-R*. Pine Bluff, Georgia. Save note."

"I should've known you couldn't use a pen and paper like any normal person," Harry teased.

"Most normal people never pick up a pen these days," Randy pointed out.

"Thanks, man. I appreciate you doing whatever you can."

"Anytime. I'll try to get back to you today with whatever I can find."

Before he ended the call, Harry asked, "Hey, I never asked—how's the new business coming? Do people actually pay you to hack into things for them?"

Randy chortled. "No, they pay me to make sure other people can't hack into their things. It's called cybersecurity. Plug that into your next internet search."

Harry smiled. "Okay. I will."

"Okay. I'm going to go finish my ride. Then I'll get on this. Talk soon."

Harry pulled the phone away from his ear and checked the screen to be sure the call had ended. If Randy couldn't dig up any dirt on these message boards, no one could.

Satisfied he'd set something in motion, Harry turned his attention to the odd bits of paperwork and scribbled sticky notes he'd left for himself on Friday afternoon. It seemed like months ago. Normally, his weekends were quiet. He spent them working, either on cases or around the house. For relaxation, he watched whatever sport was in season, and occasionally hung out with Ben or Simon. But like so many of his contemporaries, Ben and Simon had found ways to pair off, leaving Harry mostly to his own devices unless he chose to become a fifth wheel in the group.

He peeled the sticky note reminding him to pick up wine for Simon's party off his desk and studied it, his thoughts drifting back to Alicia and how well she'd fitted in with his friends. How well she seemed to fit into his life. Postkiss awkwardness aside, she slipped seamlessly into the rhythm of his household. Granted, the rhythm was more a slow, steady beat than a driving bass line, but something told him Alicia didn't mind the quiet. It wasn't much of a stretch to deduce she was as solitary a creature as him. But was it by choice or happenstance?

Slumping in his chair, he crumpled the square of paper, pondering the question. He'd always assumed he'd meet the right woman one day and get married. He'd never given his continued single status a lot of thought. Not even when ex-girlfriends sent perfectly posed photos of their angelic children. Was it possible he'd met the right woman already and failed to notice? Pursing his lips, Harry tossed the balled-up reminder into the trash. Sure. Anything was possible. And truthfully, he'd thought he'd have more of a chance with Alicia when she was in Pine Bluff in the fall. Her abrupt departure had stung, but he'd chalked his feelings up to a bruised ego rather than a hopeful heart.

Maybe he'd been too quick to dismiss them.

Sure, they'd only had the one night together, but they had worked closely with one another for the short time she had been in town. He'd liked her. Not only as an attractive, compelling woman, but as a person. He'd liked her direct manner and linear thinking. They had slotted together the chunks of information Alicia had on Coulter's activities prior to planting himself in Pine Bluff and the bits and pieces Harry had gathered—thanks to Lori Cabrera's dogged determination.

And he'd been pretty sure whatever feelings he had for her at the time were mutual. Maybe even after she left. She'd been the one who'd called the US attorney and convinced him to let Harry ride shotgun on the case. Bolstered by the thought, Harry checked the time on his phone. Deciding he'd whittled away enough of the morning to make the timing of his next call not unreasonable, he pulled up Marcus Zeller's contact information. If he was doing some additional investigation adjacent to the Coulter case, professional courtesy demanded he give the federal prosecutor a heads-up.

"Zeller," Marcus said when the call connected. "How're you doing, Harry?"

"Hey, Marcus. I'm well." His breath caught as the memory of a car bearing down on them flashed in his mind. He forced it from his lungs on a hard laugh. "For the time being."

"Well, you sound ominous, even for a Monday morning. Fill me in. What's happening?"

Harry blew out another breath and scrubbed a hand over his face. "Grab a cup of coffee—this might take a minute."

Chapter Fourteen

Alicia couldn't believe the things she'd heard over lunch at Brewster's Bakery. When Marlee texted the previous afternoon to invite her, she didn't hold out much hope for pertinent information, but figured making another appearance among the women of Pine Bluff couldn't hurt. Boy, had she underestimated the power of the ladies who lunch.

Quick-stepping it down the sidewalk, she set her sights on the municipal building, anxious to tell Harry what all she'd learned. In truth, she was relieved to have something easy to talk to him about. The previous day had been an exercise in uncomfortable restraint. Topics they didn't want to talk about far outnumbered those on the table, and the gaping holes made for an awful lot of stilted conversation. It was exhausting.

She hadn't gone back to Atlanta, obviously. She hadn't emailed Bronson or responded to his messages. Instead, she contacted Human Resources and informed them she required personal leave effective immediately. Alicia knew it was a dangerous game she was playing, but she needed time, and she needed to be involved in something other than sorting through the wreckage of what was once a stellar career. She was scared to face the possibility of finding nothing worth salvaging.

The kicker of it was, like Ben Kinsella, she had done nothing wrong. As a matter of fact, like Ben, she'd excelled at her job. But winning didn't always mean you got the prize, she reminded herself.

She checked for traffic before crossing the street, trying to keep her mind focused. But it was hard. There were so many variables. Too many pieces in play.

Her circumstances had changed radically. She needed time to think long and hard about what she wanted to do next. This pregnancy and the changes in lifestyle it would require would make it next to impossible for her to do the fieldwork she loved, even if she could get Bronson to cut her loose from her desk. And if she couldn't… If her superiors decided sitting at a desk listening to hours of unedited audio and video clips was where she would best be utilized, she wasn't sure the agency was the right place for her anymore.

Shoving her worry aside, she hopped onto the curb and hurried to the front door of the municipal building. She was excited to see Harry again, which was disturbing enough. They'd only been apart a few hours. Memories of their late-night encounter hung heavy over them. She kissed him, and he kissed her back. Then he told her things were too complicated.

And she got it. Things were complicated. Her gut told her he wasn't rejecting her outright, but it sure didn't feel good. There was something between them. It was the same sizzle she felt when they first met, but now it burned inside her steady as a flame.

Alicia tried to reason with herself. Whatever feelings she might be having toward Harry could simply be an extension of her emotional attachment to the baby she carried. No doubt he was worried about the same thing. If she were in his shoes, she would be too. Another reason she was glad to be a woman. Glad to have complete control over her relationship with her unborn child. Plus, she didn't feel overly sorry for men in general. After all, they seemed to think they should rule about everywhere else.

A rush of warm air greeted her when she stepped into the glass atrium separating the sheriff's office and jail from the district attorney's and judiciary suites. Law and justice. *Together, as they should be*, she thought, not for the first time. She started toward the door to the justice side of things. Matthew Rinker. The talk about him at the bakery may have turned into an honest-to-goodness lead, and she couldn't wait to flesh it out with Harry.

She was reaching for the door handle when the door swung open, causing her to stumble back. Catching her breath, she found herself face-to-face with the man she'd been searching for.

"Harry, I was coming to see you," she said, beaming a smile at him.

"And I was coming to find you," he replied, but his expression was anything but welcoming.

Her smile faltered, and her brow knit. "What's wrong?" She reached out and touched his arm, searching for any sign of injury. "Are you hurt? Did something happen?"

"No. I'm fine," he insisted.

"You're upset," she pointed out.

"Am I? Huh. Maybe because I spoke with Marcus Zeller from the US Attorney's Office and he tells me he heard through the grapevine you might not be assigned to this case any longer."

Alicia sucked in a breath. "Oh?"

He crossed his arms over his chest and rocked back on his heels, his steady gaze locked on her. "Yeah," he said succinctly. "He tells me one of his friends at the DEA told him you'd been put on leave. The rumors are you got crossways with your boss and you're not even supposed to be here."

"The rumors are false." She grimaced. "Or mostly false." He raised both eyebrows and she sighed. "I've taken a leave. My choice," she asserted. "Put in for a personal leave, though it's not any business of theirs."

"Personal leave?"

Alicia knew she wasn't playing fair, but she also wasn't above using every tool in her arsenal. Closing a hand over her stomach, she stared down at it meaningfully, lifted her head to meet his eyes. "Yes.

I have weeks of accumulated time I never use, and I thought now would be the perfect time to take a few days to think."

"So, you aren't on the case?"

She heard his quick intake of breath and felt a pang of guilt. This was Harry. They'd always shot straight with one another, and she had no reason to fudge the truth now.

"Technically, I haven't been since I returned to Atlanta. We have a new section chief, and he's assigned me to other things. Special Agent Morrisey is officially the contact, but Marcus Zeller and I have been friends for a long time and…" She trailed off. "As for the leave, I didn't plan to take one, but it's working out, so here we are."

"What do you mean it's working out?" he demanded.

"Bronson wanted me back in the office today. He's got no reason to want me there other than to prove he can order me to do whatever he wants me to do." She crossed her arms over her chest and mimicked his wide stance. "I don't think he's making the best use of my time or talent, so I informed Human Resources this morning I would be taking a leave of absence due to personal reasons."

"Why didn't you tell me any of this?" he asked, and the sincere hurt in his tone tore a big gaping hole in her indignation. But rather than let it show, she arched a brow at him.

"I wasn't aware I needed to consult you about my career decisions."

"You don't."

His response came so quickly, Alicia knew she'd hit a sore spot. She immediately regretted going on the offensive. Hoping to make amends, she reached out and touched his arm again, this time letting her hand close around his biceps and drawing him away from the office door. "Come on. Let's talk."

The center of the atrium was dominated by a large mosaic-tile fountain. Long drained and inactive, it still defined the lobby area. She led him to the edge of the fountain and pulled him down beside her.

"Harry, everything in the world is a mess right now for you and for me." She gave him a half smile. "But there's only one thing I'm truly happy about, and the rest I'm gonna have to let play out a bit before I make any big decisions."

His Adam's apple bobbed when he swallowed, but Harry nodded. "I get you."

"I know you do," she said, gentling her tone. "There are a lot of things hanging between us, but for right now, can we set all the other stuff aside? I have some things I want to tell you. Information I picked up, but I need to get your take on how valid you think the information may be."

"Information on what?"

"Matt Rinker," she said, holding his gaze.

Harry sat up straighter. "What about him?"

"I went to a lunch today at the bakery. Something

Marlee called the Ladies Guild?" she said, wrinkling her nose at the name.

Harry smirked. "Ah. The Ladies Guild."

"I take it you're familiar with them?" she prompted.

"My mother used to be the president."

"Okay, well, you probably have a pretty good idea of what goes on at their meetings."

"I know there's a lot of talk," he replied, a note of disdain tingeing his voice.

"Well, some of the talk today was about how nice it was to see poor Marjorie Rinker happier these days. She's telling everyone her boy—" she emphasized the word and pulled up air quotes to make it clear this was not the terminology she might have chosen "—Matthew is doing so much better since he's found the Lord."

Harry shot her a blasé stare. "This would be the point where one of us should insert a joke about how we didn't know the Lord was missing and blah, blah, blah," he said, circling his hand. "Let's take it as a given and get to the good stuff."

"She thinks his salvation will save him from the clutches of addiction."

Harry's lips parted in surprise. "Addiction? Addiction to what?"

Alicia couldn't help but feel smug about what she had to share next. "Pills. Apparently, young Matthew got himself hooked on pills. Painkillers, to be exact. To hear some of the ladies of the guild talk, there have been some unreported thefts at the pharmacy.

Carolee Masters says Mr. Rinker has been trying to get his son into a rehab center for months, but Matt wasn't having anything to do with them."

"I hate this for the Rinkers," Harry said quietly. "My heart goes out to Chet and Marjorie that they have to deal with this kind of anguish for their only child. And Matt was a good guy...at one time."

"From what I heard, it sounded like Mr. and Mrs. Rinker believe their son has found the path to the straight and narrow after attending a tent revival over in Prescott County."

Harry pulled a face but shrugged. "Whatever works."

But she wasn't done driving home the point of her story. "Supposedly, Matt became enthralled by a preacher who liked to use serpents as a part of his sermonizing."

Harry's attention had drifted, but when she said the word *serpents*, his gaze snapped back to hers. "Are you serious?"

Alicia was unable to contain the twitch of excitement tugging at the corners of her mouth. "They say he became friends with some of the gentlemen who provided the animals for these exhibitions. He was training to become a handler himself. At the Reptile Rendezvous."

She had the pleasure of watching Harry's normally impassive expression cycle through a full range of emotions. "Well, I'll be damned," he murmured.

He came around to gazing at her with something

she could only label as shock and awe. "You're trying to tell me Chet and Marjorie Rinker's son is an oxy addict who found Jesus at the tent revival with a bunch of snake handlers?"

"Exactly." She risked a small smile. "He also has a direct connection to Samuel Coulter."

"At least to Coulter's business. We don't know about the man himself," Harry corrected.

She inclined her head in acknowledgment, pressing on. "Listening to some of the ladies talk, or rather, how they didn't talk when Mrs. Rinker was around, I get the feeling people around here know more about Matt's activities than his parents."

Harry exhaled long and loud. "I feel so bad for them," he said gruffly. "I know it's ridiculous given what's been happening to me, but I've known the Rinkers all my life."

"I can understand how you'd feel…conflicted," Alicia said, though she wasn't entirely certain the statement was true.

She had never had the kind of connections with people that Harry had with the residents of this town. She couldn't quite wrap her head around how he might be feeling generous or forgiving toward any of them, but this duality between the no-nonsense prosecutor and the empathetic man was what made him so attractive to her.

Reaching over, she clasped his hand. "I'm hoping we can set things right for you with a few well-placed questions."

The door to the sheriff's department swung open and Julianne Shields burst into the atrium with Ben and Deputy Mike Schaeffer pushing past her none too gently.

"Get out," Ben snapped, dashing past them to the staircase leading to the second level, where the county offices were housed.

"Evacuate now," Mike Schaeffer yelled as he bolted into the justice side of the building.

Harry grasped Alicia's hand tightly and rose, turning his attention back to Julianne. "What's going on?" he asked, his head whipping around and his eyes following Mike and Ben.

"Bomb threat," Julianne answered, her face panic-stricken. "We need to evacuate right now," she insisted, shooing them toward the exit doors.

"Bomb threat?" Alicia repeated, moving toward the doors and dragging Harry in her wake. "Are you kidding me?"

"I wish I was kidding. Come on," she said, pushing the outer door open wide and holding it for them.

Alicia turned back to see Ben had gathered the clerical staff who worked on the second floor and was herding them down the steps. She was dragging Harry through the door when they spotted Danielle, Layla and Judge Nichols trailing Mike Schaeffer from the building.

They moved across the street onto the lawn surrounding the historic courthouse. Every one of the mu-

nicipal building's employees turned and stared at the
squat brick building in shock as Ben counted heads.

"Lori's off duty?" Alicia asked Mike.

He nodded. Pulling out his cell phone, he drew
up the other deputy's contact information and di-
aled. "She is, but I'd better let her know what's happening."

Once Ben had finished his head count, Alicia
turned to him. "Do you even have people qualified
to deal with a bomb threat here?"

He nodded. "Sort of. No bomb squad or anything,
but one of the guys on fire and rescue got a quali-
fication."

Alicia stared at him, openmouthed. "Has this person ever actually worked on a live bomb?"

Ben merely shrugged. "No cause to, as far as I
can tell. We don't get a lot of bomb threats around
here." His expression grim, he stared at the front of
the building. "This is all getting way out of hand."

Alicia snorted. "It got way out of hand a while
back."

Beside her, the sheriff nodded, but didn't take his
eyes off the building. Alicia peeked over her shoulder to find Harry speaking quietly with the judge
and the two women who worked in his office. Layla
was visibly shaken. Alicia wondered if the young
woman would stick with the DA's office after all this
madness or seek a safer position with a white-shoe
firm in Atlanta. There, she'd only have to deal with
the terrorists within while she found ways for their

wealthy clients to become even more wealthy, rather than fighting the injustices of the world.

The wail of a siren cranked up and alerted them to movement from the fire-and-rescue team. A bright red fire truck pulled from its bay and turned right onto Main Street. It roared and growled the full block and a half to the municipal building. Alicia smirked as they pulled to a halt directly in front of the doors.

"They could've run down the street," she commented dryly.

Ben proved he was still a city slicker at heart with the smile he wore when he turned to look at her. "Where's the fun in that?"

"Any ideas on who your tipster might've been?" Alicia asked while they watched a handful of firemen jump from the rig in full turnout gear.

Beside her, Ben shrugged. "Julianne says it was a woman. Said she thought she knew the voice but couldn't quite place it. Maybe once the excitement calms down and she has a minute to think," he replied laconically.

Alicia gave him an assessing stare. "For a guy who doesn't field bomb threats often, you sure are taking this in stride."

Ben met her gaze directly. "After the past couple weeks, nothing is going to surprise me." He took her elbow and pulled her along with him, moving farther down the block to get a better view around the front of the fire truck. "The sooner this damn trial starts and finishes, the happier we'll all be."

"Amen," she murmured. "But we also have to hope it ends in a conviction."

"True," he grunted. He nodded to the single man wearing full body armor who jumped down from the truck holding his helmet in his hand. "Betting Toby Bates wishes he hadn't thought it would be so cool to sign up for an explosives course," he said dryly.

"Is it me, or does he look to be no older than twelve?"

"He looks young because he is young. Joined the department straight out of high school, from what he tells me," Ben replied.

She watched as the younger man hefted a metal box she assumed contained whatever tools he might need for the task. Glancing at Ben, she asked, "You know him?"

Ben nodded. "His dad's one of the managers at Timber Masters. I've met them through Marlee, but he made a point of seeking me out not long after I got to town."

Curiosity piqued, she studied the sheriff. "Why?"

He shrugged. "Toby's parents weren't happy about him not going to college. They weren't happy about him joining the fire service either. They weren't thrilled about a lot of things I thought should make a parent proud." His jaw tightened. "Since when did protecting and serving one's community become a career choice parents discourage?"

An involuntary snort escaped her before she could stop it. Ben turned to her, startled. "What?"

She turned to face him, her expression solemn. "My relationship with my parents summed up in a single question."

He opened his mouth to speak, but the blast of an explosion ripped through the air.

Cracks appeared in the building's glass doors. In a flash, Harry was by her side, his strong arms wrapping around her. They grappled as his weight drove her to the ground. She shifted her weight to land on top of him, but soon found herself flat on her back staring up at the cloudless winter sky.

Panting, she shoved against his shoulder. "Let me up."

"No way," he huffed.

"Harry, damn it, that bomb wasn't meant for me. It was meant for you," she said, hoping to jolt some sense into him. He needed to let her protect him.

No such luck. "There's no way I'm going to let you be hurt on my account. If you won't take care of yourself for the sake of taking care of yourself, think about the baby," he said, his voice rising on the last word.

Their eyes locked and held, and in the middle of all the pandemonium, there was a beat of shocked silence. It closed around them like a bubble.

And it popped the instant Julianne Shields asked, "What baby?"

Chapter Fifteen

Harry allowed himself to be ushered along with the rest of the spectators to Brewster's Bakery, where they would wait while the law enforcement professionals combed through what evidence they could recover from the scene. No one had been injured in the blast. Toby Bates had yet to go inside, thank goodness. All around them people hovered and buzzed. Alicia had been seated at a table in the center of the room and quickly surrounded by a bevy of clucking mother hens. She sent him imploring glares, but Harry was having a hard enough time keeping his mind wrapped around the fact that somebody had literally built a bomb and left it in his place of business.

The fountain. He'd heard one of the firefighters say it blew up the fountain. For some inexplicable reason, the news made him terribly sad. Sure, it hadn't functioned in years and had become sort of a depressing eyesore, but he remembered it from when he was young. Back in the day, it had bubbled and gushed, making the spacious atrium come to life with the sound of rushing water. His dad used to give him pennies to toss into it. For the life of him, he couldn't recall a single wish he'd made with those coins, but he knew what he'd wish for now.

He wished this would all go away.

Matt Rinker. Could he have done this? Up till now, he'd been able to disassociate the notion these attacks were being perpetrated by someone he knew, but now they had a name…

"Mike, we need to take the rest of the statement in a more private setting," he said in a low voice. "Alicia and I have been putting some things together and we have some theories, but no proof. I don't want to talk about it here."

To his credit, Deputy Schaeffer simply nodded and made a note on the order pad he'd borrowed from Camille Brewster's back counter. "Absolutely," Mike replied, his tone brusque and businesslike. "I can't believe somebody put a bomb in our building."

Harry smiled at the young deputy, both in sympathy and with a wistful longing for the days when he was so certain his world was safe. "It seems like the world is getting stranger and stranger," Harry commiserated.

"I don't think the internet helps these matters," Mike said. "People get fired up over things that aren't even real. I watched a whole documentary on it on Cineflix the other night. Everyone is spouting off, and they stop seeing one another as people. The next thing you know, they're doing a damn search on how to build an incendiary device out of household goods."

Or throwing flaming bottles of kerosene through living-room windows. Harry tapped the tabletop with two fingers, then rose from his chair. "I don't want to sound like an old fogy, because I'm not one, but I agree. It seems like this is all ramping up."

Mike nodded solemnly. "My dad keeps telling me people need to remember the good old days weren't always good. A lot of bad stuff went on before. We didn't hear about it the second it happened."

Harry inclined his head, deferring to the younger man's wisdom. "You're right. And not everything you hear is true. Or needs some sort of response."

Mike's gaze traveled to the counter, a sly smile curving his lips. "Only one thing remains the same."

Harry was intrigued enough to bite. "What's that?"

"Camille Brewster makes the best darn doughnuts in all of Georgia."

Harry laughed and cast a glance at the counter himself. "A truth universally acknowledged, my friend." He raised a hand in farewell to the younger man. "I'm going to grab a couple hits of sugar, then see if I can't smuggle Alicia out of here until some of the commotion cools down. Would y'all mind coming by the house to take the rest of our statements?"

"Not at all," Mike replied affably.

Harry nodded. "Are you a jelly or cream-filled man?"

"Personally, I tend to go with a chocolate-glazed twist," Mike admitted.

"One chocolate-glazed twist coming right up."

Harry stepped to the counter where Camille was busy resetting the coffee maker. He wasn't sure if it was the excitement or the sudden rush of midafternoon customers adding the rosy glow to her cheeks. After all, one man's bomb was another woman's boom, he thought to himself wryly.

When the older woman turned, she gasped as if surprised to find him there. She pressed her hand to her heart and fluttered it a bit. "Oh, Harry, I didn't hear you come up."

"Hey, Mrs. B," he said by way of greeting. Adult or not, there were some folks in town he never could address by their given names. "Can I get a chocolate-glazed twist and two cream-filled to go, please?"

The older woman plucked a sheet of bakery tissue from the box and snapped open a bag with a practiced flick of her wrist. "Honest to goodness, Harry, I have no idea what this world is coming to."

"Seems to be the sentiment of the day," he replied tiredly. "Would you mind putting the twist in a separate bag?"

She dropped the two cream-filled doughnuts into the open sack and rolled the top down. "Not a problem." She opened a second bag, and he pulled a five-dollar bill from his wallet. Harry held it at the ready, but when she reached the register, she waved his money away. "Absolutely not. Not today." He opened his mouth to protest, and she held up a hand. "Besides, these doughnuts are hours old, and they're probably going to give you a stomachache."

She shoved the bags across the counter. Leaning in, she pitched her voice low. "Your lady friend appears to be done in. I suggest you get her out of here as soon as you can."

Harry smiled at the notion of Alicia being described as anybody's lady friend and knew instinctively she'd be insulted by the implication she was "done in." He chanced a glance over his shoulder and found the woman in question glaring daggers at him. Unable to suppress a mischievous smile, he turned back to Mrs. Brewster.

"Exactly my plan, ma'am." He nodded to the bag. "Thank you for these."

"It's my pleasure, hon. You go on now. I'll handle these lookie-loos," she assured him.

Harry dropped the five in her tip jar.

She only nodded and turned to switch out a full coffeepot for an empty one.

Harry snatched up the bags, dropped one on the table in front of Mike. Elbowing his way to the table where Alicia sat surrounded, he cast a tired smile at the crowd.

"Excuse me, folks. I need to steal Alicia, if I may." The people seated around her gazed at him blankly, and it was all Harry could do to keep from snapping at them to back off. Nodding to Alicia, he gave what he hoped was an encouraging smile. "Come on. I got something for you."

Out on the sidewalk, Harry unrolled the bag. "Mike said he and Ben would come over to the house to take our statements." He reached into the sack and used the bakery sheet Mrs. Brewster had left in there to extract one of the cream-filled doughnuts. "Here. You need to keep your strength up."

She smirked and took the pastry from him. "There you go, treating me like a cop again." She exhaled long and loud. "Thank you for the save. And for this," she said, toasting him with the doughnut.

"How well do you know Marcus Zeller?" Harry asked as they turned the corner and headed toward his house.

Alicia's brows shot up in surprise. "Zeller? From the US Attorney's Office? He's a good guy. One of the best. Why?"

"He seems oddly unperturbed by all of this," Harry said, gesturing to the street around them. "And untouched."

"You think he's in on things?"

"Not necessarily. But I worry maybe someone has gotten to someone. Or something."

Alicia stared straight ahead, her doughnut still clutched in her hand untouched. "Part of Coulter's strategy for asking for a bench trial was he didn't want a jury, right? He didn't want to be tried in the court of public opinion."

He inclined his head. "Always part of it, but people also opt for a bench trial when they think they can beat the evidence presented. The odds are stacked against the defense. The prosecution only has to convince one man—Judge Schneider. I don't know the man, but judges are notoriously harder to convince than juries. We can only sway them with evidence and the testimony of key witnesses."

"The chain of custody on the evidence is in agency hands," Alicia reminded him.

"It is."

"Are you starting to think he has the judge or someone at the DEA in his pocket?" she asked.

Harry sighed. "I don't know what to think. Someone detonated a homemade bomb in the building where I work. My house has been shot up, and my car has suffered more abuse than any vehicle deserves," he said with a wry smile. "All I know is, for some reason I'm bearing the brunt of this. None of the others involved in bringing Samuel Coulter to justice are seeing the same kind of backlash."

"Has anyone tried to bribe you?" she asked bluntly.

"No. Of course, I wasn't on their radar at first. I'm only along for the ride on this case. It's Zeller's show. I figure they thought I was a nuisance they could scare off."

"I see." Alicia nodded, taking a large bite of the doughnut. White cream oozed from the pastry. She had a smear of it on her upper lip. Harry was tempted to stop and kiss it away. The events of the day, compounded by the kiss they'd shared Saturday night, made him wonder what he was waiting for.

"We need to find a way to get to Matt Rinker. I think if we can flush him out, maybe get him cornered, he'll let us know exactly how deep this goes."

Alicia nodded, still chewing. She swallowed the bite and peeled back the paper in preparation to take more. "Agreed." They walked in silence for a few seconds. As they approached his house, she popped the last bit of her doughnut into her mouth and chewed. Pulling her phone from her pocket, she said, "I think I have an idea of who can help us."

A SHORT TIME LATER, Harry opened his front door to find Deputy Schaeffer, Sheriff Kinsella and Marlee Masters standing on his porch. He waved Mike and Ben in, but frowned at Marlee when she passed. "I wasn't expecting to see you here."

Marlee barked a laugh. "Way to make a girl feel welcome. I'm gonna have a word with your mama about your manners the next time your parents come to visit."

Harry wagged his head and shut the door. When he turned back to find her still standing in his space, he leaned forward to brush an apologetic kiss across her cheek. "Of course you're welcome. I simply was not aware you'd be joining in the fun. I thought we were giving a statement."

Marlee straightened. "You are, but Alicia texted me and asked me to come over. It seems we have a plot to hatch."

He let the notion of a plot roll around in his head while he and Alicia quickly and dispassionately recounted everything they'd noticed about the city municipal center atrium in the brief minutes they'd sat on the edge of the mosaic fountain.

Once they were finished, Ben nodded to Deputy Schaeffer and clapped him on the shoulder. "See, this is where rank pays off. Type all this up for us, will you, Mike?" he asked with a good-natured chuckle.

Schaeffer rose from his seat. "No one was going to wait for you to type it up, Sheriff. We'd all have gray hair."

Marlee snorted, turning to Alicia. "He's a two-finger typist."

When Mike left, Ben turned back to the rest of them. "Actually, I'm a good typist, but I don't want them to know. I hate writing up reports."

Marlee reached over and gave his hand a pat. "Sure you are, sugar," she cooed. Her expression turned all business. "Okay, so you need to lure Matt Rinker out into the open," she said, getting down to brass tacks. "I have an idea, but I don't know if you'll like it or not."

"Oh," Harry murmured. "This doesn't sound good."

Marlee gave a mirthless laugh. "I know you won't like it, Harry, but you'll go along with it because I'm pretty sure Alicia will see the wisdom of my plan."

He smiled. It was hard not to appreciate how much Marlee Masters had come into her own in the months since she'd taken over running her father's business. "All right, shoot."

"Well, as you may know, but Alicia may not, the live nativity starts this weekend," Marlee began.

"Live nativity?" Alicia asked, bewildered.

"We set up a stable and manger scene on the lawn outside the old courthouse and cast real people to portray different roles in the nativity."

"At the courthouse? Can you even have one on public property?"

Marlee snickered. "The courthouse has been decommissioned and is now a privately funded museum, therefore not technically government property."

Alicia processed the information. When she peeked at Harry for verification, he could only nod.

"I see. And this live nativity would involve…what, exactly?"

"Well, all the churches in town are involved. It's a devotional sort of thing. We have a Mary and a Joseph, a bunch of shepherds, an angel and, of course, a baby Jesus."

"Of course you do," Alicia murmured, her eyes wide with what Harry could only assume was shock. "People really do these things?"

"It's an old tradition. We put it on for a couple of hours on the weekend evenings leading up to Christmas. We start this weekend."

Harry narrowed his eyes at Marlee. "What are you suggesting?"

"My mama is in charge of arranging scheduling for those participating," Marlee responded with an overbright smile. "I'm sure I can convince her to let you all participate. We'll let it be known you're in, and hopefully, Matt Rinker will show himself."

It was Ben's turn to snort. "I know I must be missing something, but why would something like a live nativity lure a man out of the shadows?"

Alicia sat up straighter. "Because he's been saved," she said without thinking.

Marlee flashed her a beauty-queen smile. "Bingo!" Turning to Ben, she softened the smile but didn't dim the wattage. "Matt Rinker has found religion. And he found it at a revival where some of Samuel Coulter's snakes were being handled," she said, rolling her eyes. "Either way, he considers himself a devout Christian these days."

"Apparently, he missed the whole bit about loving thy brother as thyself," Harry said dryly.

"Or the thou shalt not kill part," Alicia grumbled.

Marlee waved a hand. "Anyhow, the Rinkers participate every year. Matt plays one of the Magi."

Harry fixed his gaze on Alicia. "When did you fill Marlee in on all of this?" he asked her.

Alicia shrugged. "She's the one I texted."

"You got it all into one text message?" he asked, incredulous.

She smirked. "Maybe I'm as good a typist as Ben is."

Marlee laughed. "I was at the Ladies Guild meeting when Marjorie was talking about Matt."

"Ladies Guild?" Ben asked.

Marlee covered his hand with hers. "I'll tell you about it later."

Alicia swallowed a laugh. "Trying to lure him out isn't a horrible idea. But we can't be certain he isn't trying to do more than scare you. My gut feeling is he's not. If he really wanted to hurt you, it wouldn't have been hard to do so in a more direct way."

"Don't forget Saturday night," he reminded her grimly.

A faint flush colored her cheeks. "Except for Saturday night."

"What happened Saturday night?" Ben asked.

Harry sat up straighter. "There was one incident we didn't report," he admitted. "The night of Simon Wingate's party, when we were walking home, a dark sedan with no headlights came at us in the street."

Ben stiffened. He slid his hand out from under Marlee's to reach for the notebook in his breast pocket. "Why didn't you report it?"

Alicia sighed tiredly. "We had no description of the vehicle, no license plate number—we had nothing to go on other than we saw a dark car coming at us. We had to make a dive for some bushes on the other side of the road."

"You're sure they were aiming for you?" Ben pressed.

"One hundred percent," Alicia answered.

"The driver hopped the curb," Harry said, taking up the story. "When he realized he wasn't going to be able to get us without mowing down half the yard, whoever it was wheeled around and took off.

Neither of us was in a position to get an ID on the car or the driver."

"Matt Rinker drives a black Camry," Marlee said almost to herself.

"What?" Ben said, swiveling toward his girlfriend.

Marlee pursed her lips. "I saw him at the Daisy driving Marjorie's car. I asked her about it, and she said they sold it to Matt so he could have reliable transportation to get a job. It's newish, but not brandnew."

Alicia fell back against the cushion of her chair and tipped her head to the ceiling. "Ding, ding, ding! Folks, we may have a winner."

"Are Marjorie and Chet in contact with Matt?" Harry asked Marlee.

She shrugged and wobbled her hand. "Sporadic. They had a big falling-out when things started to go missing from the pharmacy, and I think he used to turn up now and again trying to hit his mom up for money. But to hear Marjorie, he's completely turned things around since the tent revival. She's saying it was his salvation from addiction."

Alicia leaned forward again. "So, what are you proposing? How can we be sure this Rinker guy will show up if I put on a robe and play shepherdess?"

"Oh, Alicia." Marlee sighed. "Have you learned nothing about this town? All we have to do is let it be known you and Harry will be taking part in the nativity, and the gossip mill will take care of the rest.

Never underestimate the power of word of mouth."
She eyed Alicia with a raised eyebrow. "Anyway, I
wasn't suggesting you dress up as a shepherdess."

"You weren't?"

The surprise in Alicia's tone reflected Harry's
own. He frowned at Marlee, wary of the sparkle in
her bright blue eyes. "What did you have in mind?"

"Why, I was gonna ask Mama to cast Alicia as
Mary. After all, it seems we've had our own miracu-
lous conception right here in Pine Bluff, haven't we?"
she said, dividing a Cheshire-cat grin between the
two. "Now spill. What's this I hear about you having a baby?"

Chapter Sixteen

"I feel ridiculous," Alicia groused.

Harry adjusted the flowing piece of fleece he wore on his head. "This was your brilliant idea."

Drawing the draped blue fabric closer around her, Alicia shivered as they walked toward the town center. "I hope somebody remembers to bring a space heater."

"I don't believe they had those in Bethlehem," Harry commented mildly. "You sure you're okay with this?"

Her jaw set resolutely, she nodded. "I am ready to draw this guy out. And take him out, if necessary."

"Let's hope it doesn't come to that," Harry said briskly. They covered another half block in silence before he spoke again. "Alicia, we have a lot of ground to cover."

She nodded. "We're almost there."

"I'm not talking about the walk."

"I know. Let's get past this. We'll talk about… everything."

"Okay. But I have a few things to state for the record before we walk into this," he said firmly.

She eyed him, wary. "Okay."

"I need you to try to lie low. No one knows who or what you are other than a handful of people. No one will expect any heroics from you. There's going to be a crowd there, and I know your first impulse is to throw yourself in front of any danger. I'm asking you to think before you act."

Alicia swallowed the surge of indignation rising inside her. The implication she was a hothead who acted before thinking was completely unfair. But she and Harry had been doing the who's-protecting-who polka since she'd arrived, so maybe he had some right to ask her to rein it in. And maybe it was time they drew some firm lines.

"I promise I won't do anything foolish," she said, speaking slowly and deliberately. "But I also take exception to the notion of me thoughtlessly endangering myself or anyone around me. I am a trained professional, Harry."

"You're also a pregnant woman who may be carrying her one and only chance to have a child," he reminded her. "Likely my one and only chance too." She opened her mouth, but he raised a hand and drew to a halt. "I care about you, and I want to have the chance to see how things unfold between us."

She stared at him. How was she supposed to respond to such direct honesty? Was this what he was implying by saying this child might be his only chance at being a parent, as well?

Drawing a deep breath, she gave him a dose of her own truth. "Harry, I care for you too. I'm attracted to you, as I showed the other night. I believe there might be something more between us, and I'd be open to exploring those feelings, but I don't want this to be only because of the baby."

He inclined his head. "Fair enough. And I need you to believe me when I tell you it isn't only about the baby."

Unable to resist touching him, she reached for his hand and his fingers closed warmly around hers. "Okay, so let's catch this guy and see if we can't get on with the rest of our lives."

"Sounds like a plan," he answered.

The area set up for the live nativity was small, which Alicia figured was a good thing since there was a distinct lack of heaters available. They crowded into the open stable constructed from two-by-fours and a slanting plywood roof, and stood where Carolee Masters directed. A wooden crate with spindly crisscrossed legs attached served as a manger.

"Kneel beside it, dear," Carolee said, placing an implacable hand on Alicia's shoulder and applying a surprising amount of pressure. "And try to look adoring. You've given birth to our Lord and Savior."

Alicia stifled the urge to laugh, but a startled gasp escaped when she realized the baby doll she expected to see nested in the hay was a live infant swaddled tightly against the chill. "That's a real baby," she blurted.

Carolee Masters let out a tinkling laugh, pressing harder on Alicia's shoulder. She allowed her knees to buckle and she sank down beside the makeshift manger.

"Of course it is, darlin'. We strive to be authentic," Carolee said, waving her clipboard at a wandering shepherd to shoo him back into place.

Alicia stared up at her, stunned anyone would allow a small baby to lie exposed to the cold like this. "But they were in the desert. It's only forty degrees out here. It's too cold to keep a baby out here for hours at a time."

"Oh, we swap them out," one of the other women called to her. "Don't you fret none."

Alicia's eyes widened. She returned her attention to the contented baby sleeping through all the hubbub. "Swap them out? How many babies do you have?"

"Well, this has been a good year," Susie Troutman informed her. "We have three Jesuses all between the ages of six and nine months. We don't let them participate until they're over three months old." She wrinkled her nose. "I know he's supposed to be a newborn and all, but anything under six months is too young for the night air, you know?"

All around her, people nodded in agreement as if this reasoning were perfectly sound. Alicia saw Harry stationed near the front of the manger scene.

Other people in various homemade costumes arrived.

"Oh, good," Carolee Masters cried, clapping her hands with excitement. "Our angel has arrived, and so has our Joseph."

Alicia spotted a beautiful preteen girl with strawberry blond hair dressed in a white robe and sporting a gold tinsel halo. As Carolee fussed over the man who would play her biblical spouse, Alicia surveyed the assembly. She'd memorized the photographs Marjorie Rinker had provided and was convinced she'd recognize Matthew Rinker if he was nearby. But the only familiar face, aside from Harry's, knelt down at the other side of the manger and flashed a devastatingly potent smile.

"Hello, wife," Simon Wingate said jovially.

Alicia could not hold back her snort. "Are you kidding me?"

"We couldn't let Mary have any old husband," he said with a retaliatory sniff. "Only the best." Kneeling over the makeshift manger, he whispered, "Don't worry. I took years of tae kwon do as a child. Don't forget—I'm the one who broke Samuel Coulter's wrist."

"I remember. You're Pine Bluff's answer to Bruce Lee."

He gave her a sober nod. "Damn straight." He pulled a face when he spotted the sleeping baby. "Sorry, Jesus," he apologized completely straight-faced.

Carolee Masters directed the rest of the cast to

their places, and a small group of people assembled a few feet away from the makeshift stable. The chatter died down as the woman standing in front of the group raised her arms. They opened their mouths and began to sing "Away in a Manger."

Alicia wanted to speak to Simon but found him gazing adoringly at one of the women in the choir. She turned and squinted at the assembled singers. Deputy Lori Cabrera stood in the second row, her usually neatly coiled hair flowing like a dark river over one shoulder. Shaking her head in disbelief, she muttered under her breath, "This town."

She saw Harry's lips tilt into a smirk as his gaze locked with hers. Sometimes it seemed the man could read her every thought. In case he could, she marshaled all of her powers of concentration and sent one right back at him.

This place is too much.

His smirk grew into a full-fledged smile and she knew he'd read her loud and clear.

They sat for thirty minutes, Alicia doing her best to maintain the guise of the adoring new mother. The more she watched the child sleeping in the hay, the easier it became. She had no idea if the baby wrapped in the wool blanket was a boy or a girl, but it didn't matter. The baby was pink-cheeked and healthy, and the sight of the child tugged at something deep inside her.

She was scrolling through a mental list of all the things she would and would not allow her baby to do when someone jostled her from her thoughts. A woman stepped forward with another baby in her arms.

"It's time to switch them out," she said with a friendly smile. Nodding to the baby in the manger, she asked, "Would you mind?"

"Oh."

Alicia stared down at the still-sleeping child and her heart rate kicked up. She'd never held a baby before. She didn't have siblings or nieces or nephews. She didn't have close friends whose kids called her auntie. Never in her life had someone thrust a baby into her arms, desperate for a brief respite from motherhood. She met the woman's expectant expression, then studied the way she was holding the next child slated to portray the infant Savior.

"Yes. I can get him. Or her."

The words were out of her mouth before the reality of what she was being asked set in. Alicia hoped someone else would step forward to volunteer for the task. Perhaps this child's mother? But no one came to her rescue. Drawing a deep breath, she reached into the manger and slid her hands under the sleeping child, pulling up handfuls of straw with the baby. She cradled the child's back and head like she'd seen on television.

"How dare you lay hands on the Christ child?" a voice boomed from the back.

Shocked, the assembled residents turned toward a tall man holding a box spray-painted gold. He wore a hooded cape of deep purple velvet, but his face was thin and gaunt. Alicia recognized him in an instant. This Matthew Rinker didn't resemble the confident young man captured in his mother's photos.

The people surrounding him parted. His eyes blazed as he stepped toward her. "How dare you lay hands upon our Lord? You, a woman who lies with a man who is not her husband," he said in a voice both slurring and tremulous. He swung around to speak to the group at large, and almost as one, they took a step back in the tiny, confined space. The choir's version of "O Holy Night" drifted away.

He rounded on Carolee Masters.

"How dare you bring this whore of Babylon into our sacred adoration? Do you not know what she is?" he demanded.

To her left, Marjorie Rinker stepped forward from the crowd. "Matthew—" his mother began in a calming tone.

"And you shall cast out these demons! Listen to those who speak in new tongues," he cried.

Rinker turned his gaze on Alicia, and she could see his pupils had contracted to mere pinpricks in his eerie light blue eyes. Heroin. The man hadn't found salvation from his addiction. He'd simply found somebody who would feed both of his hungers. Samuel Coulter had done this to him, and she would make sure Samuel Coulter paid.

Moving slowly, she pulled the child closer to her, opening her fingers to let the straw fall to the ground at her knees. She hugged the baby close and turned to place her body between the infant and the shouting man. Frantically, she scanned the stunned faces around her, trying to make eye contact with one of them so she could make a subtle handoff. But they were all watching Matthew Rinker. Surely, he wouldn't try to harm her while she held the child he believed to be the son of God.

"Rinker—" Harry began, stepping closer to her. The man knocked back the hood he wore, and Alicia was dazzled by the glint of the floodlights catching the gold metallic emblems sewn into his robe. He was dressed as one of the Magi, she assumed. A king who would come to worship before an infant.

"And you," the man spit. "Don't you know the disgrace you've become? Don't you understand the work we do is holy?"

Harry took another step closer, but Alicia motioned for him to stop. "Holy in what way?"

She was on her knees holding an infant, not a doll. Certainly not the best position to take somebody out, but she could stall him long enough to mitigate the scene unfolding around them.

Out of the corner of her eye, she saw Lori Cabrera peel away from the choir and circle to the back of the stable set. Her gaze automatically sought Marlee Masters, for where the blonde was, Sheriff Ben Kinsella was sure to be nearby. Sure enough, there was an empty spot beside her new friend.

Alicia was assessing her next move when Rinker

tossed back the side of his robe and lifted his arm fully extended. He held a gun and the business end of it was trained on Harry. Her Harry.

"In my name they will cast out demons. They will speak in new tongues. They will pick up serpents, and they will drink any deadly thing. It will not hurt them. They will lay their hands on the sick and they will recover," Rinker cried, his voice rising to a fever pitch.

Alicia didn't care if Harry thought she was a reckless hothead; someone had to act. Turning to the person beside her, she thrust the now squirming child into their arms and swung back to the manger. Grasping it by the spindly legs, she swung the wooden crate upward. Straw flew everywhere, raining down on her as the side of the wooden manger made contact with Rinker's outstretched arm.

A gunshot rang out, and a chorus of wails and cries quickly followed. She swung the manger again as she rose, and this time it made a satisfying clunk when it connected with the side of Matthew Rinker's head.

Suddenly they were swarmed.

She gained her feet in time to see Ben Kinsella tackle Rinker to the ground. The assembled group closed in on them, every person desperate to see the outcome of the commotion. Everyone except Alicia. Pushing toward the front of the set, she cried his name.

"Harry! Harrison Hayes!"

She pushed her way past body after body. Where

had all these people come from? Before she could open her mouth to yell again, he appeared in front of her. His hands closed around her upper arms and he gripped her slightly harder than was absolutely necessary, but she couldn't blame him, given the circumstances.

"You said you wouldn't do anything reckless. You promised you'd think of the baby," he ground out from between clenched teeth. His lips grazed her temple. She was sinking into his embrace when he thrust his arms out, pushing her away again. "Damn it, Alicia, you promised to think of our baby."

Our. Not *the* or *your*, but *our* baby. Who knew a simple pronoun could mean so much?

"I was thinking of the baby," she whispered against the fleece fashioned into his shepherd's robe. "All I could think of was how much our baby needs a father."

HIS HOUSE WAS CRAWLING with people. Not only were Ben, Lori and Mike taking statements for the sheriff's department records, but also a guy named Alan Campbell, from Alicia's department at the DEA, had been dispatched to gather information on what was happening. At first, he thought her boss sent someone to check up on her. The man's presence got Harry's hackles up, but he seemed to be an ally. He'd driven down to Pine Bluff on his own time to pass on some information. Harry was relieved when Alicia seemed happy to see the guy. From what Ben had told him, her current section chief wasn't the easiest person in the world to work for.

Thankfully, Marlee Masters had arrived on his doorstep and taken dealing with the extraneous pieces of this circus out of their hands. She'd swooped in with a coffee maker under one arm and bags of snack food dangling from her fingers. With the brisk efficiency of the CEO she was, she shooed any nonessential hangers-on out the door, put Simon Wingate on refreshments duty and graciously offered the use of a Timber Masters rental home to Special Agent Campbell, effectively dismissing him, as well.

Harry thought things were wrapping up when the doorbell rang one more time. Excusing himself, he checked through the newly replaced sidelight, and a tangle of disbelieving laughter caught in his throat. US Attorney Marcus Zeller was standing on his doorstep at nearly nine o'clock on a Saturday night.

"News sure travels fast," he said by way of greeting. He stepped back and ushered the other man in. "Come on in. I have a new coffee maker and they're cranking it out in there. No one will be sleeping tonight."

Zeller smiled and stepped past Harry into the foyer. "I don't mean to intrude, but I heard what happened and I thought it might be better if I came here in person so we could speak face-to-face."

Harry ushered him into the deserted living room. As usual, everyone had congregated in the kitchen. He couldn't blame them for avoiding this room. The stench of kerosene still lingered in the air, and they'd had to order glass to replace the broken window, so the view was mostly plywood.

Zeller took it all in, before taking a seat on the sofa. Harry couldn't help but think of how Alicia had perched on the same seat the night she'd shown up at his house out of the blue. She'd sat there with her chin tipped up in defiance, but her voice carefully controlled. She came here to tell him she was pregnant with his child. Until now, Harry hadn't truly realized how what had seemed like a shocking disruption in his life had grounded him rather than turned his world upside down. Rinker brought the chaos. Alicia brought the calm.

"Harry, I hate to do this after all you've been through in the past few weeks," Zeller began.

Harry held up his hand to stop the other man. "I'll be asking to be removed from the case."

Zeller blew out a breath. "Man, I hate this. You have every right to be sitting on this case, but…"

Harry shrugged. "But," he said, as if the conjunction had magically transformed into punctuation.

"I want to assure you the chain of custody on the evidence is solid. We have more than enough to convict Coulter."

Harry wanted to believe the other man's assertion wholeheartedly, but he couldn't help but wonder why Coulter would forfeit his chance to sway more than one person. The judge alone…

"I also wanted to inform you Judge Schneider has asked to be recused from hearing the case."

Harry blinked in surprise. "He has? Why?"

"It turns out the judge isn't wholly unconnected to what has been happening here." He tipped his head toward the rise of voices coming from the other room and pitched his lower. Harry had to lean in to hear. "The judge is Matthew Rinker's uncle."

Harry's eyes opened wide. "Excuse me?"

Zeller nodded. "Marjorie Rinker's brother. Her maiden name was Schneider," he explained. "The judge claims he had no knowledge of what was happening here with you and his nephew, but given the circumstances, we all agreed it was best he removed himself from the case."

"Holy—" Harry scrubbed a hand over his face, staring at Marcus again in disbelief. "Are you serious?"

"I wish I weren't. But you know how it is around here, Harry. It's not unusual to have relations spread all over the county and beyond. Folks generally don't stray too far from home."

"True," Harry said. He took in the living room where he'd watched television with his parents and sister growing up. Sure, the place looked completely different since he'd renovated, but it was still the home he'd always known. Shaking himself from his reverie, he tried to focus on the practicalities. "What does this mean for the trial?"

"The trial will go on as planned. We've asked for

a change of venue. We'll try him before Judge Mc-
Intosh in Macon. He's made room on the docket so
there will be no need to postpone. I'll be taking a
second chair on from within my own department."

"Wow. Okay. You sure can get a lot done fast."

"Harry, I want to assure you I'm going to do
everything in my power to convict Samuel Coulter
on the evidence and put him away. We'll be charging
Matthew Rinker in federal court, as well."

Harry's head jerked back. "You will?"

"The cases are tied together. One of the guys over
at the DEA uncovered some proof Coulter's been in
communication with Matthew Rinker."

"Alan Campbell." Harry let his eyes drift up to the
ceiling. "I can't believe all this was going on right
under our noses."

Zeller snorted. "Well, you've been distracted. We
all thought this was the usual petty stuff surrounding
a high-profile case. We didn't see something bigger
happening here, and I apologize. We should have dug
deeper the first time you called and told me you were
getting vandalized. But you know how it is. This stuff
comes with the territory."

Harry's lips thinned into a grim line, but he bobbed
his head in agreement. "Yeah, it does."

A sudden burst of laughter came from the kitchen,
and Harry wished he was in on the joke, whatever it
was. He hated not being in there. Hated being separated from Alicia even for a brief time. They had far
too much to iron out.

Slapping his knees, he rose and offered his hand to Zeller. "Thank you for coming to tell me in person. I hate you had to drive all this way at this time of night to do it, but I appreciate the effort."

"It was the least I could do." Zeller clasped his hand. "And don't think I won't be calling you, you know, in case I need to get some particulars once the case starts rolling."

"It would be my pleasure. Nine days and counting," he said.

"Nine days and counting," Zeller repeated. Then he cracked his first smile. "We've got him, Harry. We've got him, and we won't let him get away."

"All I need to hear."

Chapter Seventeen

Alicia sensed Harry's approach. When he appeared, he stood in the doorway, staring at them each in turn as if trying to get a sense of what he'd missed. Alicia tried to see things through his eyes. She, Ben, Lori and Marlee sat in the chairs surrounding his kitchen table. Mike Schaeffer stood hunched over the counter, scribbling notes and shoveling a steady stream of chips and salsa into his mouth. Simon Wingate leaned against the counter, a bottle of beer in his hand and his trademark smirky smile lifting the corner of his mouth. He stared at the back of Lori's head, clearly smitten.

Alicia envied Mike his ability to eat. For once, her queasiness had nothing to do with the baby and every-thing to do with the echo of a gunshot in her mind. Her stomach had been tied in knots since the second she realized she couldn't see Harry at the front of the set.

She hadn't been kidding when she said she wanted their baby to have its father. What was more, *she* wanted their baby's father.

"Guys?" she said, interrupting some playful bickering between Marlee and Ben. The room fell instantly silent. "If you don't mind, Harry and I have some things to talk over, and it's getting late."

Almost as one, they rose or straightened, murmuring about their own need to get home. Lori and Marlee extracted a promise she'd meet them for breakfast at the bakery the following morning. Knowing she couldn't put their interrogation off entirely, she agreed.

She stayed put at the table as Harry showed them out. Snippets of conversation drifted back to her, but she was too tired to piece them together. Closing her eyes, she tipped her head back and forced herself to take three slow breaths. The edge of panic in Harry's tone jerked her from her meditation.

"Are you okay?"

She exhaled, lifting her head, and met his concerned gaze squarely. "I'm fine. It's only… If there's going to be any more talking tonight, I think it needs to be you and me."

He tipped his head to the side slightly, as if needing to translate her words. Then he moved so fast he became a blur. He stood beside her, but rather than taking the seat Lori had vacated, he reached for her hand and pulled her up. Alicia was half-afraid he was going to go all protective but distant on her again. Peck a gentle kiss to her forehead and lead her to the guest-room door with promises to talk more when they were thinking clearer. But she didn't want promises or protection. She wanted—

His mouth.

He pressed his mouth to hers in a kiss so ardent it almost hurt. Before she could catch on, he broke away and pulled her hard against his lean body. "Damn, I was so scared," he murmured into her ear. "I couldn't see you, and I was so scared."

"I couldn't see *you*. I was scared for *you*," she corrected, turning her face into his neck. If she was settling for a hug, she was going to take a big hit of his scent while she could. "For us," she added.

"I know." He ran a soothing hand over her hair. "If anything had happened to you and the baby—"

She cut him off right there. "I wasn't scared for the baby." When he pulled back slightly, she winced. "I mean, yeah, I was scared for the baby. Of course I was. But it's not *the* baby, it's *our* baby, and I needed you to be okay so I can ask you…" She trailed off, heat rising inside her.

Before she could stuff her embarrassment back down, he spoke. "Ask me anything."

"Do you want to take a chance on seeing if there can be an *our*— An *us*, I guess," she corrected.

"Yes," he answered with gratifying swiftness. "Yes. Definitely."

She tipped her face toward him. "You'd better kiss me again. Like you mean it. And if you try to tell me this is too complica—"

His lips were on hers before she could finish the word. When they parted, breathless, he peered into her eyes. "I'll go to Atlanta if you want."

Taken aback, she peeled away to search his eyes. "What?"

"I can get a job with the DA's office up there, or maybe even see what they have going at the Department of Justice. Aside from Zeller down here, I know one of the US attorneys working out of the northern district offices—"

She pressed her fingertip to his lips to stanch the flow. "Do you want to leave Pine Bluff?" she asked, genuinely dubious.

He shrugged. "I'll go anywhere."

Alicia stared at him in amazement, wondering what had happened to the cautious, skeptical man she'd encountered a few weeks before. "I wouldn't ask you to move."

"But your career—"

"But *your* career," she countered. "Besides, mine has not been going the way I'd like it to," she admitted. At his puzzled frown, she sighed. "Harry, what you saw here in the fall was a fluke. I had an opportunity under a chief who wasn't threatened by a woman who is too good at her job, and I took it."

"How can someone be too good at their job?" he asked, genuinely perplexed.

"By standing out. By showing up the other people on her team, rather than playact at being one of the guys." She scowled. "I won't apologize for being the best they had, but I won't be punished for it any longer."

"Punished for it?"

"Relegated to research or scouring through hours of surveillance. The only reason I caught the Coulter case was because I was the one who traced and tracked him. I was the only one who thought he was the one. They thought I was on a wild-goose chase, but I proved I wasn't. How did the agency reward me? They promoted the guy who gave me the chance and brought in another guy determined to keep me tied to a desk so I don't dare show up anyone else."

"That's ridiculous."

"That's bureaucracy," she countered. "If the agency can't appreciate excellence, I will find a place where people do. Maybe someplace like Pine Bluff."

"Alicia." Her name came out in a tortured whisper. "I can't ask you to move here."

"You aren't asking—I am," she said, lifting her brows to drive home the point.

"But Ben's department… There's no budget for anyone else, and you're grossly overqualified to be a deputy."

"But I'm an excellent investigator. Surely I can cobble together some sort of career."

"Sure, but is this what you want? You've worked so hard—"

"And it's gotten me nowhere," she concluded. "But the leave of absence buys me some time to think. What if I wanted something different? What if I don't want to be chained to a desk or married to my job? What if my parents were wrong, and life is about more than the constant pursuit of excellence?

Excellence has gotten me a set of credentials I rarely get to use. Some meaningless commendations, an empty apartment and no friends to speak of."

She paused, her finger tracing the grain of the table where she'd sat surrounded by people she'd come to think of as friends. "I don't want to be perfect. I want to make magnificent mistakes," she said, pulling his hand around to press it to her belly. "There has to be more. I want more."

"There is," he assured her, his hand pressed to the slight curve of her stomach. "There already is."

"I want a place to call home. Someone I can count on. Friends who come running with coffee makers, chips and salsa."

"They're your friends too."

"I want you," she said simply. "Who knew I'd discover so much when I came to Pine Bluff to arrest Samuel Coulter?"

Harry's smile was slow to unfurl, but when it stretched fully across his face, the effect was astounding. "Special Agent Simmons, you had me at *I have a warrant.*"

* * * * *

 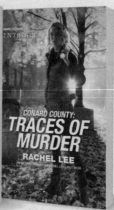

#2031 TEXAS STALKER
An O'Connor Family Mystery • by Barb Han

While fleeing an attempt on her life, Brianna Adair is reunited with her childhood friend Garrett O'Connor. Trusting others is not in her nature, but Brianna will have to lean on the gorgeous rancher or risk falling prey to a stalker who won't stop until she's dead...

#2032 STAY HIDDEN
Heartland Heroes • by Julie Anne Lindsey

Running from her abuser is Gina Ricci's only goal, and disappearing completely may be the answer. But local private investigator Cruz Winchester wants to arrest her ex and set Gina free. When everyone in Gina's life seems to become a target, will Cruz be able to save them all...without sacrificing Gina or her unborn child?

#2033 ROGUE CHRISTMAS OPERATION
Fugitive Heroes: Topaz Unit • by Juno Rushdan

Resolved to learn the truth of her sister's death, Hope Fischer travels to the mysterious military-controlled town where her sister worked at Christmas. Teaming up with the enigmatic Gage Graham could lead to the answers she's looking for—if Gage's secret past doesn't find and kill them first.

#2034 K-9 PATROL
Kansas City Crime Lab • by Julie Miller

After his best friend's sister, KCPD criminalist Lexi Callahan, is attacked at a crime scene, K-9 officer Aiden Murphy and partner Blue will do anything to protect her. But being assigned as her protection detail means spending every minute together. Can Aiden overcome his long-buried feelings for Lexi in time to save her from a killer?

#2035 FIND ME
by Cassie Miles

Searching for her childhood best friend requires undercover FBI agent Isabel "Angie" D'Angelo to infiltrate the Denver-based Lorenzo crime family. Standing in her way is Julian Parisi, a gentleman's club manager working for the Lorenzo family. Angie will need to convince Julian to help even though she knows he's got secrets of his own...

#2036 DEADLY DAYS OF CHRISTMAS
by Carla Cassidy

Still recovering from a previous heartbreak, Sheriff Mac McKnight avoids Christmas at any cost, even with his deputy, Callie Stevens, who loves the holidays—and him. But when a serial killer's victims start mirroring *The Twelve Days of Christmas*, he'll have to confront his past...and his desire for Callie.

YOU CAN FIND MORE INFORMATION ON UPCOMING HARLEQUIN TITLES, FREE EXCERPTS AND MORE AT HARLEQUIN.COM.